Love Letters & Gingerbread

An Annapolis Christmas

LOVE LETTERS & GINGERBREAD

An Annapolis Christmas

Mary K. Tilghman

FOXHALL BOOKS

BALTIMORE

© 2019 Mary K. Tilghman
All rights reserved. No part of this book may be reproduced, stored in a retrieval system or transmitted in any form or by any means without the prior written permission of the publishers, except by a reviewer who may quote brief passages in a review to be printed in a newspaper, magazine, journal or on-line post.

First edition

This is a work of fiction. Names, characters, businesses, places, events and incidents are either the products of the author's imagination or used in a fictitious manner. Any resemblance to actual persons living or dead, or actual events is purely coincidental.

ISBN: 978-1-7338792-2-4

Published by Foxhall Books, Baltimore

www.maryktilghmanwrites.com

Printed in the United States of America

LOVE LETTERS & GINGERBREAD is printed in Baskerville.

FOR
GINA, SEAN AND BRIGID

To Jane Austen
who inspired this story

Chapter 1
Letters

"Patsy! You have a letter!" When Patricia heard that happy news, she closed her book and skipped down the stairs. Angela, sitting at her desk with the day's mail, held a small white square aloft.

"Thank you." She plucked it from her sister's fingers and quickly glanced at the handwriting. It was, as she hoped, from Vincent. She lovingly caressed the big loops and decorative capitals of his penmanship.

Then giggling with delight, she clutched it to her bosom and ran to the sun-warmed window seat across the room from her sister. Her constant companion, a little brown and white dog named Timmy, jumped up beside her.

She stroked his head as she sat for a moment to study the page that so recently had been in Vincent's hands. She relished the idea that he had thought of her, dreamed of meeting her again, longed to be by her side. Then, as the heat of a pink blush rushed up her face, she tore open the letter.

Though Vincent Stewart lived only four doors away, he thrilled Patricia with these tiny declarations of love several times a week.

But this one was different. She knew immediately. It was short, addressed only to Dear Patricia. Why didn't it say "Dearest?" she wanted to know.

She quickly scanned the few lines he had written and gasped. None of it made sense. He was leaving? For Frederick? Until the New Year?

"Oh Vincent, how could you!" Patsy's voice was filled with despair. Little Timmy hopped up and stared at her, his tail wagging.

Angela looked up from her correspondence. "What is it, dear?"

Patsy was sure her sister couldn't possibly understand but she had to tell someone. She crossed the drawing room floor and dropped onto the chair beside Angela's desk. "Vincent is going away. He'll be gone until the New Year." She sighed heavily and looked back at the letter. "And I've been knitting the perfect Christmas present for him. His mother's family invited them to spend the winter in Frederick."

Her mood became blacker as soon as she realized something terrible. "He won't be here for the Winter Ball."

"Oh, Patsy. Your first dance and he won't be there."

Patricia smiled weakly at her sister's concern and then folded the letter with a frown. "I can't imagine why they're going away now."

She stood to put the note in her pocket before wiping her damp eyes. "At least he promises to write while he is gone. That is something."

"Won't you see him before he leaves?"

Patsy shook her head. "He's leaving tomorrow. He says his parents have him running errands for them as they get everything packed for the journey. So our carriage ride with his mother yesterday was the last time I'll see him in 1831. It will be 1832 before I see him again."

"It's only three months," Angela said.

"Nearly a hundred days. That's a long time without the love of my life." She sighed again. "I better go write a farewell note." She trudged out of the drawing room, every step heavy as she climbed the stairs. Timmy raced after her, his little paws clicking on wood floors.

A knock on the front door stopped Patricia in her tracks. Perhaps Vincent had come. Perhaps he was coming to say goodbye in person.

She flew down the steps and swung open the door. A brisk autumn pulled at her curls as she came face to face with its author.

"Mr. Stewart!" Patricia was breathless as she took in the sight of the gentleman. He stood there with his broad-brimmed tan hat in his hand, wearing her favorite tailcoat in a silvery shade of gray.

"May I come in? It's quite cold today." If his tone was sharp, Patricia refused to notice. Her dog, who stood at her feet, growled and ran for his pillow in the drawing room.

She took his hat and held it to her heart as she gazed at the curly brown hair and fiery dark eyes she loved so much.

Recalling Angela was busy with the bills, Patricia wrapped her arm around his and suggested he accompany her to the kitchen. "It's much warmer there. Perhaps you'd like a cup of tea?"

Once she had put down his hat on the kitchen table and set the kettle to boil, Vincent gathered her up in his arms. "I'm so sad to be leaving you, dearest Patsy."

Patricia nearly swooned in his embrace, to hear him use her given name, to feel his warm arms about her. "So am I, Mr.—" She giggled a little and blushed. "So am I, Vincent. You won't be here for Christmas or New Year's. Or for so many things. Not even the Winter Ball."

Steam rose from the tea kettle and she invited him to take the chair by the fire while she filled the teapot.

When the hot kettle was safely on its hob, Vincent captured her hand in his and pulled her to him.

The tea forgotten, Patricia ignored the rules of propriety and threw her arms around him. "I'm going to miss you." She whispered the hot words into his neck.

Vincent turned his head to kiss her cheek. "Will you write?"

She nodded. "Every day." Then she pulled away with a look of worry. "But I don't know where to send the letters."

"I thought of that," he responded with a slight smile. From the tiny pocket of his waistcoat he retrieved a small square of paper. "My aunt and uncle's address is here."

Patricia crushed the paper in her fist and hugged her beau again. "Getting a letter from you every day won't be the same as having you here, but it will help."

When he didn't respond, Patricia concluded he must be overcome with emotion. She allowed them to remain entwined in silence for as long as she could. The sound of footsteps forced her to step away.

"Patsy, who was at the door?" Angela stopped at the entrance to the spacious kitchen when she saw Vincent. "Oh, hello, Vincent," she said. "I understand you are spending the holidays in Frederick. We'll miss having you around here, won't we, Patsy?"

Patricia blushed. "Vincent gave me his address in Frederick. I told him I would write." She smiled and cocked her head at her beau who took her hand and squeezed it.

"I really must be going now." He bowed slightly to Angela. "Mother has a thousand errands for me to run before we leave in the morning."

"Oh, no. So soon?" Patricia was crestfallen.

"Mother thinks I'm on my way to the market. That will take half the afternoon so I knew I could fit in a few minutes with you."

"I'm so glad you did." Patricia smiled again, though she held back tears that burned her eyes. She didn't want Vincent to see her as anything but happy and completely in love. She hoped for some tender word of affection from him. But she knew Vincent wouldn't chance such a thing in the presence of her sister.

"Did you want something?" she asked Angela. "I just made some tea."

"Yes, I could do with a—"

"Oh, well, then. Let us get out of your way. I'll walk Vincent to the door." Hoping her sister would keep busy in the kitchen for a few minutes, Patricia picked up Vincent's hat and took his arm.

One tear slipped down her cheek as they reached the entrance hall. She leaned against him and let the warm, soft wool of his coat soothe her face. How would she be able to bear so long a time without him near? She almost asked him until a noise from the kitchen made her stop.

"The holidays won't be the same without you," she said instead. "I was so looking forward to the Winter Ball. I've been dreaming of dancing every dance with you."

"I'm sorry, Patsy." Vincent's dark eyes looked directly into hers and she was sure she could see disappointment there. "But now I must go."

He eased his hat out of her grip, letting his hand rest on hers a little too long. "Farewell, my dearest." He rushed down the front steps.

"Dearest." She echoed Vincent's last word in the faintest of whispers as he hurried away.

Little Timmy stood at her feet, looking up with his liquid brown eyes.

She stooped down to pick him up and nuzzle his soft fur. "Are you my dearest?" she cooed. "Of course you are. Would you like to come help me write my letter? You would?"

Then with a giggle, Patricia gathered her skirts and she and her little dog swept up to her bedroom. She had to write this very instant. She wanted her love to have a letter waiting for him when he arrived in Frederick. She would miss him terribly all through the winter, but she was determined that he never forget her.

With Timmy resting at her feet, she put her pen into the ink pot. Her hand shook as a sudden thought troubled her: There might be distractions in Frederick that Vincent wouldn't find at home. Her letters would be more important than ever.

She had to be sure he remembered his one true love waited for him, patiently in Annapolis.

Chapter 2
Not guests, visitors

As Patricia ran off to write her letter to Vincent, Angela carried her teacup into the drawing room and set it on the green leather inlay of the desk. She had put off attending to her correspondence long enough.

As much as Patricia liked receiving mail, Angela had, in the past year, come to dread it. She used to handle her father's bookkeeping and correspondence for his medical practice and now she was learning where his generosity had led the family. He had forgiven the bills of those who couldn't pay, accepted chickens and melons and squash as payment enough or took a few coins even when the bill was much higher. He believed there would always be time to make up the difference.

The trouble was, he had run out of time. When he died and she took over the household ledger, Angela discovered a pile of debts. And unlike her sweet father, these creditors weren't in a forgiving mood. Father's accounts had to be settled and with her mother still grieving, the task was up to her.

Now, staring at a new stack of bills and letters from lawyers, she missed him and worried what was to become of the family.

Angela bit her lip and unfolded the first letter. When she saw the lawyer's signature, she braced herself for more bad news, holding her breath and reading each line carefully.

She gasped as she studied the letter. Father's many debts had been resolved.

There was sad news, too. "Dr. Richard Edwards has agreed to buy the house," the lawyer wrote.

She'd known this was a possibility but seeing it finally arranged took her breath away.

She looked around the sun-drenched room where the family had always gathered. So many Christmases had been celebrated here, the Tannenbaum always beside the fireplace. Patsy and she learned their letters and practiced their penmanship here. This was where they spent every evening of their lives. It was a warm place, full of love and family.

There had been sadness here, too. She was sitting with her mother and sister when word came that Father had been stricken. It was in this room, a little more than a year ago now, that his body was laid out for his funeral.

Though her heart was full at the realization that their days in this house were at an end, she had done her best to prepare herself for this resolution. Of course, she had tried to come up with other ways to pay off the bills. Sometimes, she had to admit, she'd found herself full of anger or resentment that her father's decisions had led them to this point. When their lawyer assured them that selling the house was their only choice, Angela dried her tears and began looking for a new place to live.

Though she was going to miss this house, and this room most of all, Angela knew from the past year's experience how much work it took to keep a townhouse this big running. Relocating to smaller quarters was a sensible decision. But that didn't make it any less difficult. Though no date for their move was set, Angela knew it would be soon. Perhaps before the New Year.

With a heavy sigh, she rifled through the rest of the mail. Her vision blurred as she put aside letters from her Uncle Karl in Sharpsburg and Uncle Max on the outskirts of Annapolis. Letters filled with family news were the one pleasure her mother still enjoyed and so Angela always carried them up to her room without opening them.

The last letter came from Richard T. Edwards, M.D., the new owner of their house. She held her breath as she scanned it quickly, curious about why he was corresponding with them now.

She jumped from her chair. He was coming today! At eleven o'clock! She glanced at the clock on the mantel. Goodness, less than an hour away. She quickly read the rest of his letter. He was bringing his wife Henrietta and their younger son, Gordon. Just a short visit, he assured them. Gordon, who was usually away at school, had never seen the house and Henrietta wanted to ask a few questions.

Angela had to hurry. She looked around the room with a critical eye. No one could criticize her housework; everything was in order.

She had only one worry as she gathered up the mail.

Her mother may not be ready to receive guests yet. In her grief, she had not yet picked up the mantle of hostess. She moved much more slowly since Father's sudden death, living more in her past than in the present.

Angela decided to take care of a few other details before checking on her mother. Her visitors might enjoy a welcoming repast.

She bustled into the kitchen to add water to the kettle and browse the cupboards, looking for a bite to eat. Patsy had baked her favorite sweet rolls for breakfast. She put aside two on a plate for her mother and then assembled the rest under a linen towel. They would do, Angela decided. She assembled cups, saucers, plates and napkins on a tray, ready for their guests.

That bit of preparation satisfied her. She tucked the mail under her arm, picked up a cup of tea and the rolls to take to Mother's chambers.

Angela rapped lightly on her mother's door before easing it open and greeting her in a soft voice. "Good morning, Mother."

She found her mother awake and sitting up in bed. Her eyes were red and she clutched a crumpled handkerchief. Angela hoped for what had to be the hundredth time that one day she would love someone as deeply as Mother still loved Father. Twenty-four years of marriage and her ardor had never dimmed.

"We're having company today," Angela began. "I wondered—"

"Today? But I'm not ready to receive visitors, Angela." Mother put her hand to her nightcap.

"I'll help you get ready. It's Dr. Edwards who's coming, Mother. He's agreed to the terms of the sale." Angela hated to be the bearer of bad news. Like Patsy, her mother could be quite excitable.

Olivia Harris closed her eyes to take in the news. "Why does he have to come today? What could he possibly want?"

Heaving a heavy sigh, she wiped her eyes and climbed out of bed. "Do we know what time he'll be arriving?"

"Yes, Mother. He'll be here at eleven." Angela stooped to pick up the quilt that had fallen to the floor and pull it across the bed.

Her mother turned from the highboy, a look of worry in her eyes. "Do you mean to say he might be here shortly?"

"Everything is in order." Angela picked up stockings and the nightcap her mother had dropped.

Before she turned for help lacing up her corset, Mother smiled with pride at her elder daughter. "I can always count on you, dear Angela."

Angela's heart swelled at her mother's gratitude. But time was a-wasting. She helped her mother into her petticoats and skirt, adjusted the bodice and then hurried her mother to her dressing table. "Here, let's attend to your hair. I brought you a few letters you might want to read, too."

She laid the letters on the table as her mother coiled and pinned her long hair. "These are from Max and Karl."

"Max and Karl." The worry in Mother's face faded away. "I'll put these away for later. We must get ready."

"I think you have time before the Edwardses arrive. I know you haven't heard from your brothers in quite a while." She finished her sentence with a pat on her mother's shoulder.

"Yes, of course." Mother's reflection in the dressing table mirror smiled back at her daughter. Angela always considered her mother the prettiest woman she ever knew. Her eyes were the same gray-blue as Angela's though a year of mourning had dulled their luster. Her blonde hair was thick with threads of silver running through the gold. Angela always envied her mother's coloring. Instead of pale golden locks, Angela's hair was a reddish-brown, like Father's. She didn't know who Patsy looked like with her dark brown hair and eyes.

Angela finished pinning her mother's hair while she scanned Dr. Edwards's note and opened her brother Max's letter. After a quiet moment spent reading, Mother turned in her chair and thrust the page at Angela. Her expression shone with relief. "We have a place to live!"

Then she crushed her handkerchief against her mouth as tears slipped down her cheeks. "There's no other solution, is there?"

LOVE LETTERS & GINGERBREAD

Angela wrapped her arms around her weeping mother, laying her cheek against her mother's soft head. "I'm afraid not. Much as I wish we could stay, this is for the best."

"Yes, well." Mother sat up and dabbed at her eyes. "We have talked about this often enough." It was no use. She leaned her forehead on her hand and let the tears fall again.

"Mother," Angela whispered. "If it's too difficult, let me meet with the Edwards family. I'll tell them you are indisposed."

"No, no. That would never do, Angela, my dear." She put her handkerchief aside and smoothed the hair at her temples.

As Mother pinned her brooch at her neck, Angela scanned the note from her uncle: Max, a lifelong bachelor who kept a small house on the west side of Annapolis, invited the family to move in with him.

"What do you think of Max's offer?" Mother asked.

"It's awfully far out of town, isn't it?" Angela blurted out.

When her mother shot her a withering look, Angela wanted to climb under the bed. But she meant what she said. Uncle Max's house was in the middle of nowhere. Their house on Prince George Street was only a few blocks from the harbor and mere steps to all their friends and their favorite shops. Uncle Max lived on the edge of town where the best view was of tobacco fields. She couldn't imagine what Patricia would say when she heard the news.

"You and your sister will love living there." Her mother looked at the letter again, a rare smile on her face. "What a generous man your uncle is. He says the house is nearly always empty and we can make it our own. He does spend an awful lot of time in his shop, poor dear." She bit her lip as she studied the letter a moment more. "The minute Dr. Edwards and his family have left, we will sit down and write to Max to accept his wonderful invitation."

Angela nodded. There was never any further discussion with her mother once she had decided. "Yes, Mother. That sounds like a sensible decision."

Her mother put a forefinger to her chin and looked out the window for a moment before speaking. "Best not to tell Patsy yet. She's so smitten with her young man. Something may come of that soon."

"I doubt it." Angela frowned. "It seems Vincent is going away."

"Whatever do you mean?"

"Patsy just got some bad news. He is leaving with his family to spend the winter in Frederick. He was here a few minutes ago to say goodbye. He told Patsy he didn't know anything about it until today."

"Is he leaving so soon?"

"Tomorrow."

"Oh poor Patsy—"

A knock at the front door interrupted their conversation. Mother's hand flew to her hair as she bent to check her appearance in the glass. "Let me finish dressing."

With a flush rising to her face, she asked her daughter to go meet the family and offer a cup of tea. "Do we have any scones? Biscuits? Well, whatever we have, offer a plate of them to go with the tea. Tell them I'll be with them shortly."

"Of course, Mother. Drink a little of your tea, too. I'll take care of our guests for a few minutes." She stopped and remembered Patsy. She hadn't had time to tell her sister the news.

As her mother scurried around to tidy the chamber her daughter had already put in order, Angela went to her sister's room. Patsy needed to know before she could go to greet their ... what were they? Not guests, exactly. Visitors, then.

Chapter 3
Dearest Vincent

Patsy stared at the empty white sheet of stationery and pondered what to write. Vincent was leaving. In the brief time she had known him, Patsy came to rely on his unwavering attentions. He never seemed to be far from her. Until now.

Vincent had brought a bright light to a year so full of turmoil as she and her family adjusted to life without dear Father. What a terrible year, it had been. Father had gone so quickly. And that had led to many changes, including the prospect of moving to another home.

Her eyes roamed from her letter paper to the scene outside her window. Even the view was changing. The poplar tree across the street blazed a glorious gold.

"Dearest," Patsy whispered, recalling Vincent's farewell. Now he was bringing change of his own.

She couldn't get her mind to settle on the words to write. She wandered around the room, finally laying her hand on a book of poems. A blue ribbon marked the last poem she read. A pretty thing, she stopped to reread it.

Love's eyes are so enchanting, Bright, smiling, soft and granting …

Mr. Woolworth had spoken the truth. She dropped back into her chair and picked up Timmy, snoozing under the desk. The paper, still empty, waited for her.

She didn't want to write a letter at all. She was tired of sitting and waiting and wondering. In truth, she wanted to run down the street and beg Vincent not to go. She wanted to open her heart to him. How would she bear the long winter months without him?

She hugged her pet. "I know better than to do such a thing. I have more pride than that, don't I?" she murmured to Timmy. He licked her face. "Begging is beneath me, isn't it?" He licked her face some more. "You are right as always."

She loved Vincent. She was certain of that. He was so kind, handsome, tall and elegant. He had lavished attention on her since they met during the summer at church. Newly arrived from school, it had been his first opportunity to extend his condolences on the death of her father. Then, after speaking a few minutes he asked if he might call on her.

Having him by her side eased her grief. Just when she thought she would never smile again, Vincent came to assuage her crushing loneliness, lighten her sadness with his gentle smile and happy conversation, and distract her from the constant bad news that seemed to follow the funeral.

And now, he was leaving town! She never expected such news. Not when they had grown so close. Though he never said it, she was certain he must love her as she loved him. She longed for a declaration and perhaps some discussion of their future together. None had yet come, even though his attentions to her were constant and always welcome. She'd even let him kiss her.

They'd never quarreled. Except once. And that had been over her dog. Neither dog nor man liked the other at all. But that didn't really matter, did it?

Patricia couldn't think of any time she displeased him or his mother. Mrs. Stewart, in fact, seemed fond of her. She greeted her with a friendly smile and always asked about the family. And she knew Angela and her own mother were quite taken with him.

So why was he leaving so suddenly?

Patsy leaned her cheek on her hand and watched the yellow leaves dance in the afternoon breeze. The letter remained unwritten.

The weather was a little too chilly for strolling, Though the day was sunny and bright, a stiff breeze ruffled the vibrant autumn leaves of the trees beyond her window. Still, there were plenty of passers-by. Businessmen hurried down the street, followed by a clutch of giggling girls. She looked to see if she knew them. Of course, she did. They were once classmates of hers. As they passed by the house without even a glance, she suddenly felt lonely.

She'd ignored her friends from the moment she began seeing Vincent. In a town as small as Annapolis, everyone knew all the gossip. Her friends, Jemima and Charity, at least, were aware of her attachment to Vincent. And they were more than a little miffed when she started refusing their invitations so she could spent time with her new beau. Girls didn't take too kindly to friends who passed them over for a boy.

This being her first suitor, she hadn't known there were rules. So there were her friends, Jemima, Charity, and three others, passing her house without a thought about her. Or, she feared, even worse, with only a mean thought about her.

Never mind, she told herself. She needed to write her letter to Vincent. She must assure him she would be waiting for his return and to promise him that not another man would interest her at the ball. She had her heart set only on him.

She shook the loneliness weighing on her shoulders and kissed her little dog before dipping her pen in the ink.

"Dearest Vincent," she began anew. Pouring out her deepest emotions in the most flowery prose she could muster, she covered one page and then another before she finally put down her pen. As the ink dried, she reread it. Satisfied, she sealed the letter with a kiss.

She wondered how long it took a letter to reach Frederick. And how long its response would take to return to Annapolis. Vincent would be so far away. She couldn't imagine how she'd survive a day without even one letter from her love.

Patsy wanted to post the letter straightaway so it, along with all her assurances of love and fidelity, would be placed in Vincent's hands as soon as possible. As she reached for her hat, there was a rap at her door. She sighed at Angela's voice.

"What is it, Angela?" she asked rather impatiently when she saw her sister. "I want to send my letter to Vincent."

"It will have to wait." Angela bustled past her sister. "I must go see to our visitors waiting at the front door but before I do, there's something I must tell you."

Angela's face took on a serious expression that made Patsy's heart stop. She reached for the edge of her bedroom door for support. "Has something happened? Is Mother—"

"No. No. We have guests."

Patsy sighed in relief. "Is that all?"

"No. I'm afraid they're coming because…" Patsy didn't like the pained look that crossed her sister's face.

She rushed to Angela's side. "Who's coming?"

"The house has been sold. The new owners are here now."

Patsy collapsed onto her bed. "Sold?" She had known it was a possibility but now, oh no, now it was really going to happen. They would have to leave the only house the family had ever known. She could hardly comprehend it.

Angela nodded. "I must go see to them. I mustn't keep them waiting. Patsy dear, I know this is a shock. I can hardly make sense of it myself. But we've talked about the possibility. Now it has come true. It will be all right. Uncle Max has offered us his house."

Trust Angela to be practical. If she explained with any emotion at all, she spoke with resignation. She could be so reasonable even when the world they knew was torn asunder.

She laid a hand on Patsy's shoulder, a gesture of comfort, though it had no such effect.

Then Angela rose to leave. "I hope you'll come down and greet our visitors."

"Of course." Patsy's voice was hoarse. The last thing she wanted to do was greet those people, no matter who they were. They were taking the house away, forcing her and her family to move away.

Patsy glanced around her room, with its old but lovely damask drapes, fine mahogany furniture and Timmy snoozing under her writing table.

When she sighed, he awoke and ran to her. "Did you hear?" She rubbed the dog's silky ear. "We have to move away."

Hearing unfamiliar voices in the hall, Patsy sighed. She'd promised to go down. All right then, she would go, but she wouldn't like it. Not one little bit.

Chapter 4
Gordon

Angela greeted her visitors with a curtsey. She had met Dr. Edwards several times when he visited the house to consult on cases with her father. A stout man with curly gray side-whiskers and a red button nose, he would have been pleasant to look at if he smiled once in a while. His wife, Henrietta, was as stout as he and a head shorter. Her face was even sterner than her husband's.

"Good morning, Miss Harris." Dr. Edwards bowed formally. "May I present my wife and son?"

"Thank you for seeing us on such short notice, Miss Harris. I do apologize for inconveniencing you and your mother but I had to be sure Gordon saw the house while he was home from school." Mrs. Edwards glanced at her very tall son.

Gordon towered over both his mother and father. With blond, almost white, hair and sky-blue eyes, he seemed to glow. How did those two parents give birth to such a handsome son? Angela couldn't resist her unkind thought as he flashed a dazzling smile at her. She was entranced.

Like his father, he bowed.

"Miss Harris. It is so good to make your acquaintance," he said in a gentle baritone voice.

Angela offered a welcoming smile. "My mother is looking forward to greeting all of you but is otherwise occupied at this moment. She asked me to offer you some tea while you wait."

"That won't be necessary," Mrs. Edwards was curt. "This is hardly a social call."

"Mama." Gordon leaned down to his mother. "I think a cup of tea would be a capital idea."

"Yes, Henrietta. Please." Dr. Edwards put a hand on his wife's arm as he smiled graciously at Angela.

"Well, all right." Mrs. Edwards sighed as she acquiesced. With a frown, she swept into the drawing room and looked it over with a critical eye. Then, she brushed the settee's silk damask upholstery before settling herself and her voluminous skirts.

Patricia appeared at the door, a forced smile on her lips. Then, seeing Mrs. Edwards's unwavering scowl, a look of horror crossed her face. It was brief—Patsy knew her manners—though it lasted long enough for Angela to see it.

"Patricia, please entertain our guests for a moment while I see about the tea." Angela suspected her sister would have preferred to help her rather than entertain such an unpleasant woman. It didn't matter. Angela knew she could count on her sister's outgoing nature.

She hadn't even reached the hall when Mrs. Edwards began grilling Patricia about the neighborhood. Patsy answered easily, launching into descriptions of their neighbors, better than either Angela or her mother.

"I thought you might like a bit of help." Angela was surprised to hear a masculine voice behind her. She turned as Gordon followed her toward the kitchen. "Please forgive my mother. She sometimes forgets herself when she has a lot on her mind."

"Oh? Of course. She must have a great deal to do before moving here." Angela was surprised as she felt a sob catch in her throat. Their departure from this beloved house was no longer a "someday event." Today her mother would set the date with Dr. Edwards and they would begin packing their things for their own move to Uncle Max's house. She steadied herself as she led Gordon into the kitchen.

The tea things were already prepared. Angela had remembered her mother's many lessons about entertaining guests. She poured hot water into the waiting teapot and handed the tray piled with plates, cutlery and the sweet rolls to her visitor.

"Thank you." She smiled up at her guest. "It is so kind of you to offer to help."

"Not at all. It's most selfish of me. I've been looking forward to meeting you. Your father used to talk about his two daughters with such affection."

"My father?" Her heart thumped at the thought of her father speaking about her and Patsy. She didn't remember Father ever mentioning Dr. Edwards's family. During her days helping out in the office, Angela overheard many of the doctors' conversations, all of them strictly business. Her father never discussed her and Patsy and she couldn't recall a single conversation about Mrs. Edwards or their son.

"Why yes. When I was a boy, I often listened to them talk when your father visited to consult with Father on some case or another. I have heard about you two girls most of my life."

"I wonder why we have never met until now." Angela picked up the teapot to return to the drawing room.

"I should confess that it was I who suggested to my mother we come for a visit. It all happened much more quickly that I expected and for that I do apologize." Gordon's cheeks turned a rosy pink. "My mother is a woman of action."

Angela smiled. "I suppose that is a good thing. She knows what she wants and she gets it."

Gordon's laugh was dry. "That is certainly the truth." He paused. "I was hoping, perhaps, while our parents meet, that you might show me around a little. I hear your garden is quite lovely."

Surprised by his attentions, Angela agreed. "I'm always happy to show off my little piece of the world. But it's hardly an estate. Our garden is only big enough for a short stroll and even then there isn't much to see this time of year."

When they returned to the drawing room, Angela saw with relief her mother had made her appearance. Mrs. Edwards was boasting about the accomplishments of her sons. John, she was explaining, worked in the White House with President Jackson.

"And here's Gordon. He's going to make a fine lawyer." She puffed up with pride as she gazed on him. "I insisted he study law at William and Mary instead of going to that old medical school in Baltimore. I think he'll be much happier."

A dark look passed over the Gordon's fair face as he set down the tray. Angela wondered if Mrs. Edwards's ability to get what she wanted extended to her sons' futures.

She needn't have worried about keeping up her side of the

conversation. Mrs. Edwards barraged them with a stream of opinions about everything from her children's education to the latest policies issued from the White House.

Patricia caught her sister's attention and directed her eyes toward Gordon with a smirk. Angela wanted to laugh when she saw his smile was pasted on, a testament to his experience spending time in drawing rooms with the ladies.

"Now," Mrs. Edwards stood up as soon as her teacup was empty. "I think it's high time we see about the house."

Patsy and Angela collected cups and spoons while their mother led the Edwards family on a tour. Mother's voice was tinged with pride as she guided them through the townhouse's spacious rooms and pointed out its high ceilings, intricately carved moldings and mantelpieces and fine, old furnishings. All of it would soon belong to a new family.

Angela thought of the secretary desk that had been her father's and a wave of gratitude swept through her. Mother had insisted it not be included in the inventory for the sale. Instead, it would go with them to their new home.

"I saw the way that gentleman looked at you." Patsy interrupted her reverie. As always, she sought out hints of romance in every situation.

"I was surprised when he followed me into the kitchen." Angela brushed off her suggestion.

"His mother may be looking over the house but I think he's interested in its residents. One of them in particular." Patsy chuckled. "Have you met before?"

"Never." Angela told her sister about the conversation in the kitchen and his request for a tour of the garden. "I told him there really isn't much to see."

"It depends on what one wants to see, doesn't it?" Patricia's smile was positively wicked as she picked up the empty cake plate.

Angela had to laugh as she carried the tea things back to the kitchen. Maybe Patsy was right. Nothing would surprise her today. The whole morning had been so peculiar. She had no doubt it would become even more so before it was over.

While her mother sat at the dining room table with Dr. and Mrs. Edwards to go over details of the sale, Angela returned to the secretary to finish a letter and her sister sat in the window seat to scribble lines of a new poem.

"How do you like this line?" Before Patricia could read it aloud, Gordon entered the room.

"Forgive my intrusion." He blushed. "I was wondering if Miss Harris might be free to show me the garden."

He looked from one girl to the next. "Perhaps you'd like to join us, Miss Patricia?"

Patsy smiled and shook her head. "Thank you but I think it's a bit too cold for a stroll."

"I hadn't thought of that." He turned to Angela with a quizzical look. "If you think you would be uncomfortable, we needn't go out."

"I'm made of tougher stuff than my sister." Angela was delighted to have an opportunity to enjoy the day's crisp fall weather. She would, however, remember to thank Patricia later for the chance to spend time alone with their visitor.

The garden behind their townhouse looked a little dreary so late in the season. The herb garden with its fragrant rosemary and lavender still made a nice showing but the roses had wilted on their thorny vines and an early frost had turned almost everything else a drab brown. She was glad the maple tree still retained its scarlet leaves.

When they reached the whitewashed bench at the far end of the yard, Angela invited Gordon to take a seat. "The view of the house is nice from here."

She felt a little wistful sitting beside him, looking at the house. Built in the previous century of sturdy brick, it was a tall, stately home with room for servants as well as a family. Now, only the two girls and their mother resided here. And in a few weeks they, too, would be gone. This would be his house, not hers.

Angela sighed, flooded by the many memories she and her sister had made in this garden. She thought of the games they'd played here, the languid afternoons spent reading, talking and dreaming. She'd picked flowers for her mother from these beds. She'd tripped and broken her arm near that maple when she was a reckless seven-year-old. There would be no more memories made here.

"I presume you are looking forward to living here." She had to say something to break the awkward silence. Gordon sat stiffly beside her, his hands folded over his crossed knees. When she spoke, he started and then smiled at her.

"I think it is a nice house but it really won't be where I live for more than a few weeks of the year. I spend most of my time in Williamsburg, you know."

"Yes, of course."

He looked at her with kindness. "I presume you are not looking forward to moving from here."

Angela appreciated his sensitivity and shook her head. "I will miss it very much. I've lived here all my life. But things change, don't they?"

"Don't they?"

There was something in his tone that made Angela want to know more. She knew she shouldn't pry but his words seemed an invitation to ask.

"What do you mean? If you don't mind my asking."

Gordon chuckled quietly. "I've seen a lot of difficult changes. Even before my father decided to buy your family's house."

He stopped for a moment. "You don't want to hear my grumbling."

"Oh, but I do." Angela wanted to poke at him until he told her everything. She didn't know why she was so interested. But everything he said fascinated her. She begged him to go on.

"I had my heart set on the medical college in Baltimore. You may have heard my mother mention it. I asked my father if I might go into practice with him after I earned my degree and he had agreed"

That dark look reappeared on Gordon's face and Angela leaned in sympathetically as he continued.

"Then my mother told me about the college in Williamsburg and its fine reputation. Thomas Jefferson studied law there and she thought if it was good enough for a president, it was good enough for her son. So, even though I have no interest in the law, that's where I am. Mama insisted her sons should not have to endure the long difficult hours of a doctor."

"Couldn't you just say no?" Angela felt sorry for him.

Gordon chuckled again. "Only my father says no to Mama. My brother John and I rarely attempt it. Once she has formed an opinion, it is the law of the land."

"Was buying the house her idea?"

"No, that was Father's. He said he always loved coming here and he thought long and hard about buying it. I'm sorry, of course, that it will mean you must move away."

Patsy came scurrying down the path, a shawl twisted around her shoulders.

"Your parents are ready to go." Patricia looked from Gordon to Angela with a knowing expression. Then she hurried back toward the house and left them to share another few moments alone. Angela was grateful to her little sister.

"I hope we'll meet again," Gordon said, tucking her hand in the crook of his arm. "Perhaps when I return from school I might call on you?"

"I think that would be lovely."

"You do?" Gordon's surprised expression changed to delight. "Oh that's wonderful. And may I write to you?"

"Of course. I'll make sure you have our new address once we are settled."

Gordon patted her hand affectionately as they made their way back to the house.

Chapter 5
William

"I can't believe we have to live here." Patricia collapsed back onto the four-poster bed she was going to have to share with her sister. While she absentmindedly stroked the head of her snoring dog, she looked up at the old-fashioned canopy above her, allowing her eyes to follow the swirls of the gathered fabric.

She felt a little guilty, knowing she should be unpacking her trunks. She didn't care, however; her life was falling apart and she could find no way to stop it. "We might as well have moved to the Eastern Shore. This house is so far from everything."

"Don't say that. Would you have preferred living across the Chesapeake Bay? A ferry ride away from everything and everyone we know?" Angela looked up from the letter she was reading, trying, as usual, to be the voice of reason.

Patricia appreciated her sensible sister but certainly didn't understand how she could remain calm and practical at a time like this.

Her sister went on, as she was wont to do. "We did have an invitation to rent a small cottage on a plantation near Chestertown. I am so glad Uncle Max's letter came before Mother had a chance to consider moving there."

Patricia didn't have time to respond before there was a knock on the bedroom door.

Mother held the door ajar as she finished speaking to the housekeeper. "I think that's a grand plan. Thank you, Ella," she said before the tall woman with the chocolate brown skin hurried down the stairs. Timmy hopped off the bed and scurried after her.

Then Mother burst into the room with a wide smile on her face. "Girls, Uncle Max has asked our neighbor to tea."

Patsy rolled over onto her belly and leaned on her elbows. "Who?"

"William Taylor. You've met him. He stopped while the carriage was being unloaded."

Patsy turned over onto her back and crossed her arms. "Oh, that old fellow. That should be delightful."

Mother frowned at her rude response but Patsy didn't care. She still wasn't happy about leaving their beautiful house. Even worse, she was miserable that she hadn't received a single note from Vincent. She didn't want to admit that she might also be a little envious of her sister who always seemed to be reading a new missive from Gordon.

"That's enough of that, miss." Her mother's tone was stern enough to compel Patsy to sit up in a more ladylike fashion. "Mr. Taylor is a lovely man. He's not some old fellow to dismiss so easily. He's like a son to your uncle and, since the death of his wife and baby, he really could use some friends."

"His wife died?" Angela looked up from her note with a troubled expression. "Oh…"

"Max says it's been some months but Mr. Taylor is only now feeling better. It must be awful to lose a wife and a baby at the same time."

A cloud passed over her mother's face but quickly disappeared when she caught sight of the paper in Angela's hand. "Another letter? He certainly spends a lot of time writing." Angela blushed before folding it to tuck in her pocket.

Mother turned her gaze on Patricia, still lounging on the bed, and her smile faded. "Would you be so kind as to tidy up a bit before coming down? They should be here any minute."

Without waiting for an answer, she disappeared, humming an old tune as she departed.

Patricia, a little chastened, was relieved to see Mother returning to her former ways. During preparations for the move, her mother cast off her mournful look even though her clothing remained as black as ever.

At last, Mother's eyes danced as in the old days and she smiled almost as much as before.

Patricia had always found an ally in her mother. Both of them were easily caught up in the emotion of a poem, the sorrow of an old ballad, the affairs of the heart. Patricia was glad when her mother approved of a possible match with Vincent. And, like Patricia, her mother was sorely disappointed when the young man went away.

"I wonder who the 'they' is," she asked.

"I'm sure I don't know. Mother only mentioned Mr. Taylor." Angela studied her face in a hand mirror and smoothed the curls by her face.

Patricia dragged herself off the bed and peeked into Angela's mirror.

"May I borrow that? You already look beautiful." She nudged her sister who handed over the little looking glass with a sisterly scowl.

"I'll see you downstairs." Angela left her sister alone.

Patricia wasn't happy with the face in the mirror. It looked tired, even sad. There were pale shadows under her dark eyes. And her hair, brown and dull, would never be as lovely as her sister's chestnut tresses. She pinched a little color in her cheeks and smoothed back an errant lock that fell over her eye.

"That'll do," she said to no one in particular before putting down the mirror. Heading downstairs, she heard unfamiliar voices.

The man talking to her Uncle Max had to be their neighbor. Patricia listened from the hall for a moment.

They spoke as old friends were wont to do, finishing each other's sentences, regaling each other with stories much embellished with the passage of time.

Mr. Taylor looked to be about the same age as Uncle Max, perhaps a few years younger. Patricia had to admit it was hard to tell the age of men older than their twenties. He might not be exactly handsome, but he was tall and dark, with an engaging smile. He stood erect as a soldier, which, Patricia recalled, he had been. Uncle Max once told them his neighbor and he served together in the Battle of Baltimore during the War of 1812.

Perhaps Uncle Max was interested in pairing his sister—their mother!—with his friend. Before Patricia could consider the notion further, she heard a laugh, the laugh of a girl she didn't know and couldn't see from her vantage point in the hall.

Her indifference was replaced by curiosity. She must find out what Uncle Max was up to and who owned that cheerful laugh. She entered the parlor, forcing herself to smile and remember her manners.

"Good afternoon." She spoke as sweetly as she could as she dipped into a curtsey.

The two men stopped talking and the stranger bowed most formally.

Uncle Max made the introductions, first of the girl, Jane Luness, and then of the man, William Taylor.

"Mr. Taylor is my partner in business and my favorite neighbor." Uncle Max clapped his friend's back. "I thought you might like to meet a young lady about your own age. Jane lives across the street. I hope the three of you will be great friends."

Patricia decided that her uncle might be correct. Jane had an open face and a quick smile. And it didn't take long before Patricia realized the girl might never stop talking. Or giggling.

As engaging as Jane's chatter was, Patricia couldn't keep her attention off her mother and the two men. She was curious to see if there was any flirting going on. She couldn't decide whether she should be interested or perhaps scandalized that such a pairing was possible when their father had been in his grave hardly a year.

Still, she kept up with Jane's conversation. She was a font of information who seemed to know everything about their new neighborhood. Patricia only grew bored as the talk turned toward eligible bachelors in the area. She certainly didn't need to worry about that. Vincent might be out of town but he remained in her heart.

As her thoughts wandered away from the conversation, Patricia sensed she was being watched. There was definitely a warm spot between her shoulders she couldn't dismiss. She wanted to turn but, no, she didn't want to be rude.

She fortified her attentions on the feminine conversation, eager to learn about the people and places near her new home.

When tea was served, Patricia realized her original notion—that

Uncle Max hoped for a match between her mother and Mr. Taylor—was completely wrong.

Instead, she was horrified to see, it seemed he thought one of his nieces would be a good mate for his friend. Patricia's heart sank as he invited Mr. Taylor to sit between Angela and Patricia. It sank even further when Mr. Taylor's attentions toward her never let up all afternoon. Not once did he turn to speak to her sister. It wasn't only rude, it was alarming.

Oh, he was polite to Angela and he carefully followed the conversation of Uncle Max and Mother, but again and again he turned to draw her into the conversation. This would never do, she thought as she waited for her tea.

She was relieved when Ella placed the teapot in front of her mother and offered her a plate. "Thank you, Ella. These look quite scrumptious."

Ella smiled. "I was happy to get some oysters at the market this morning. I decided to fry them up for today's tea."

"Miss Ella can turn every meal into a feast." Uncle Max's eyes shone with pride.

"Thank you." Ella nodded slightly at the compliment before leaving.

If Patricia thought changing the subject would lessen Mr. Taylor's attentions, she was mistaken.

He resumed his quizzing as she poured milk into her cup. "My friend says you are quite a dancer."

Patricia offered him the sandwich plate. "Uncle Max said that! I've hardly had an opportunity to dance in the last year. Since my father's passing, you understand. But I do love it. Do you dance, Mr. Taylor?"

Where was this going to lead? Patricia didn't want to know. What she really wanted was a few minutes to dash off a letter to Vincent. Because she hadn't received a letter from him since the move, she was convinced he hadn't learned of her new address. Perhaps the mail was slower in the winter. Maybe there had been snow or ice to delay its delivery.

"Miss Patricia?"

Oh no, she realized, she had stopped listening to Mr. Taylor.

"I'm so sorry," she apologized. "You were saying?"

"It wasn't important." Patricia saw the tiniest hint of sadness in his eyes and felt guilt thread its way into her heart.

Patricia had to try to make amends. "Your question about dancing called to mind the Winter Ball. I'm afraid my thoughts strayed. You see this will be the first ball I am old enough to attend. I had to miss last year's…"

"Ah, I do understand." The smile returned to Mr. Taylor's face. It was a nice smile. It made the laugh lines at the corner of his eyes crinkle—and remind Patricia he was much too old for her.

"I have not attended the ball in many a year," he added. "But this year, perhaps, I will go. Perhaps your mother might permit me to escort you?"

"That's so kind of you." Patricia tried her best to be non-committal. She didn't want her new friend Jane—who seemed to delight in gossip—telling everyone she and Mr. Taylor were forming an attachment.

Tea dragged on until afternoon became evening. Before it was over, Mr. Taylor had invited them to dine on Sunday and Jane and the two girls had planned a visit. Then, they waved goodbye and watched as a full moon lit the way for Mr. Taylor and Jane.

"A splendid tea, Max. Your housekeeper does know her way around a kitchen." Mother led the way into the parlor after her brother shut the door.

"Quite right." Max picked up his pipe. "When she bought her freedom, I hired her right away. Her former owner was sorry to lose her."

"Thank you for inviting Jane." Angela took her seat beside her sister. "I think she will be a great friend."

"And how did you like my friend William, Patsy?" Max added as he puffed on his pipe. As a wreath of smoke ringed his round face, a mischievous grin appeared that Patricia didn't like.

She knew she had to be kind but she didn't want to encourage such match-making from her bachelor uncle. What, after all, did he know about romance?

"He was quite nice." She picked up her book of poetry, determined to remain neutral.

"I think he was quite taken with you," Max confided.

Patricia blushed and dropped her book. "Oh, Uncle Max, I think you are imagining things. Mr. Taylor was just being polite to the new girls."

Her uncle didn't say another word but he chuckled a little and glanced at her mother as he enjoyed his pipe.

Yes indeed, she thought, Uncle Max is hoping for a romance. And he wasn't thinking of her mother at all! He was aiming for a match between that old man and her. She thought of Vincent, who was never far from her heart.

"If you will excuse me, I think I'll write a letter to my beau. I want to tell Vincent all about our tea today." She emphasized his name. "About Jane, about how you and Mr. Taylor fought during the war, oh and everything."

She picked up her little volume and strolled out of the room.

She hoped that would make clear her romantic leanings. She already had found love. How could she possibly need the attentions of that old man?

Up in her room, Patricia sat at the little table by the window and picked up her pen. A sheet of paper was already waiting. "Dearest Vincent," she wrote.

After staring at those words for a moment, Patricia looked out the window where the full moon cast a silvery sheen on barren fields. If she were a painter, she'd love to paint that scene—the color, the feeling. What words could she use to describe it?

Patricia wasn't interested in thinking about Mr. Taylor but she found it painful to turn her thoughts to an absent suitor.

She had nothing left to write to Vincent about. She'd already told him everything. She'd burnished the truth about her happiness to a warm sunny glow but the truth was she felt cold as the moonlight.She wondered with a shiver if Vincent's affections were as empty as that patch of farmland. A growing fear he was taking her fidelity and her love for granted washed over her.

Gone nearly a month, he hadn't taken the time to write to her even once. She looked at the page before her and scratched out Vincent's name.

"Pale moonlight illumines…" she wrote. Poetry always made her feel better

Chapter 6
An afternoon visitor

Angela and Patricia huddled around the kitchen fireplace with their mother. Their chairs were drawn close to the fire to chase away the chill of the cold winter's day as they tended to their mending.

Angela pulled on a thread as she reattached a lost button to her coat. Between stitches, she blew on her fingers to warm them. She said not a word and couldn't have anyway since Patricia had refused to yield the floor since they'd gathered here after breakfast.

Patricia darned a pair of stockings as she described the poem she had recently finished writing. Her creative endeavors often made her overly loquacious. She barely took a breath before moving on next to relate a visit with Jane the previous day and then to ask her mother and sister about plans for Christmas dinner.

Not a word about Vincent, Angela observed. There was a new lightness in her voice as if she'd made a decision about her absent suitor.

"Ouch!" Patricia scowled after poking her finger with the darning needle. She wiped away a droplet of blood with her handkerchief. "I wish I could throw these old things out and buy some new ones."

Her mother just looked at her. Patricia knew better than to suggest such a thing. Like Angela, she knew very well how tight money was. There was little extra to spend on niceties such as hair ribbons and new hosiery. Apparently feeling guilty for her outburst, she stretched out her handiwork to show the others. "I'm being silly, I suppose. At least I'm getting better at darning."

Her mother stopped to examine her stitches. "Yes, my dear, it looks quite good."

Patricia rolled up the mended stockings and craned her neck to see out the window. "Mailman is here." She tucked the needle in the spool of thread before she threw down her sewing basket.

"I hope there's a letter." Mother's gazed followed Patricia hurrying to the front door.

"You mean from Vincent. He hasn't sent a single one since we came here." Angela sighed. She was beginning to think he was a terrible scoundrel. After so many months of constant attention, why would he simply stop all communication with her sister?

"Poor Patricia." Mother listened for a moment before turning to stir the pot of stew Ella had left simmering over the glowing coals.

Patricia trudged back into the kitchen and handed the short stack of letters to Angela. She dropped down on her chair and crossed her arms. Then she sighed heavily. The light-hearted Patricia of a moment ago was gone; in her place was a pining Patricia.

"I have been trying to be sensible about this. But it's no use. I want to know. Why hasn't he written?"

She sighed again. "I write every day, sometimes twice. He certainly knows where we live now. He knows I miss him. He knows…. Well, everything."

"Perhaps you need to give him the silent treatment," Angela suggested as she thumbed through the letters.

"I could never play games like that." Patricia, whose emotions were always written clearly on her face, looked horrified.

"I only think, well, it doesn't matter what I think." Angela struggled to find something comforting to say to soothe her sister's pain but came up empty. Though she had little experience with men, she knew what loneliness felt. Having a suitor ignore her sister must feel horrible.

"Ah," she said, stopping at a note addressed with a masculine hand. Gordon's.

She had expected that when Gordon returned to Williamsburg he would forget all about her. Instead, he had been faithful in his correspondence, writing once a week, sometimes more. She had come to look forward to his letters, filled with observations about his classes and classmates, the weather and how he was spending his free time.

The constant attention had an effect on her heart she hadn't expected. She cared for Gordon in a way she never thought possible.

She tore open the letter and felt the paper, thick and smooth, so lovely in her hands. It was covered with carelessly scribbled letters and blotted ink though the lines were straight and even, and the correspondent had filled every inch of the sheet. Angela glanced at the signature before she read even the salutation.

"Yours, Gordon." Yours! Angela was thrilled to read such an intimate word and hungrily read the rest of the letter.

The chatter of her mother and sister faded away. She didn't hear the crackle of the fire or shiver at the chill in the air as she hungrily scanned the letter.

"He's coming." Angela looked up from the page.

"Who's coming?" her mother asked.

"Gordon is coming. He'll be in town for a few days and he wishes to come and visit." She read the page again, surprised there was no date or time for their meeting.

"Oh hurrah!" Patricia's eyes danced as she snatched the letter from her sister. "He doesn't say when he's coming! From the looks of his penmanship, he wrote so quickly he forgot to include some vital information."

Patricia handed the letter to her mother. "Oh Angela, I'm so happy for you."

Angela couldn't stop the smile or quell the thumping of her heart. Although she had found him amiable enough on their first visit, with each new letter, she found herself longing to see him again.

She endured a few minutes of chatter about the rest of the mail and a few comments about Gordon's visit. Then she sought solitude. She wanted to re-read the letter, savor that beautiful sign-off, and then respond with a note of her own.

After she tucked the letter in her pocket, she quietly gathered up her sewing kit and mumbled an excuse about taking her mended coat to hang in her armoire.

When she got to her little room, she forgot all about the coat, dropping it without a care on the edge of the bed as she turned her attention to the letter. She ran her hand across the messy address as she hurried to her chair to reread the letter. The nib of the pen had clearly been stabbed into the paper, causing blots and streaks. He smeared the wet ink as he wrote each line. She didn't expect such carelessness from such a fine gentleman.

Patricia was right, Angela concluded as she scanned the sentences. It must have been written quickly. She wondered why he was coming home after saying he was so busy with his studies. It didn't matter, really. He was coming to see her and that was quite enough.

Until now, Angela had never had a gentleman come to call on her. She had hoped for a suitor when she was Patsy's age. As the years passed, however, she stopped hoping once she realized she was getting a little old for most of the eligible bachelors she knew.

Her heart skipped a beat as she read. Gordon didn't fill his note with flowery or romantic nonsense. It was sensible, requesting her indulgence with him for a visit during his time at home. At home, she thought. At her home, now in the possession of Gordon's family. The thought didn't hurt as much as she thought it would.

Any pain she nursed was alleviated by the gentle words of Gordon's letter. Especially the way he signed it. "Yours."

Angela sighed again and then shook off the tinge of excitement the word induced. Surely she knew better than to read too much into such a simple word. After all, he might sign letters to close friends and relatives that way all the time. Signing this letter with such a word meant he did care for her a little though, didn't it?

The contents of the note thrilled her even more. Gordon was requesting a visit with her. This kind of attention would have had Patsy swooning for all to see.

Angela stroked the smooth paper and bit her lip. She was surprised how her heart danced beneath her stays.

She stared out the window a moment, waiting for her heart to settle. Outside the scene was gloomy, with only a gray sky and bare fields to look at, but inside as the fire in the hearth spread its warmth, memories sitting beside Gordon warmed Angela's heart.

She retrieved a sheet of letter paper from her desk drawer. Each time she wrote to Gordon she felt the same excitement as the first. He was the first man she'd ever written to besides her uncles. Oh, she had seen Patsy write dozens of letters to her beau, biting the end of the pen and screwing up her face to fashion a sentence full of romance.

How would she answer him? Angela bent her head to her task.

Dear Mr. Edwards,

She looked at those words. She wondered for a moment if perhaps they were too formal. But she had never yet called him Gordon. She looked at her letter again. He had called her Miss Harris.

Yes, she decided Mr. Edwards was quite correct. At least for now. Maybe one day—no, she shook the idea from her head. One step at a time. There was no good reason to read more into this than a friendly vislt.

Angela was still composing her letter when her sister called to her from the hall. "You won't believe who has just arrived." Patsy burst into the room and ran to the writing desk.

Angela, used to her sister's emotional displays, finished the sentence she was writing.

"Stop that this instant." Patricia pulled the note from under her sister's hand. "You don't need to write this because the gentleman has just arrived on our front door step. I have to add that he's terribly embarrassed his letter only arrived a few minutes before he did. So now, do your best to look beautiful and then rush downstairs. He clearly isn't interested in talking with me!"

Angela couldn't make sense of her sister's words. Gordon was here? But how could that be? She dropped her pen and put her hand to her hair. She'd hardly taken much time arranging it this morning. It must look a mess.

"Put this on," Patricia ordered. She held out one of her own gowns, a pretty thing, an ivory frock with rows and rows of dainty red roses. "It will look beautiful with your red hair."

"I do not have red hair," Angela objected. "It's auburn."

"Don't argue with me. Put this on."

Angela slipped out of her brown dress, an old toile frock so worn she only wore it when she was home. It would never do for guests. The dress Patsy held out to her was too fancy with all that extra needlework around the cuffs and the neckline scooping across her shoulders like that—well, it was too daring. She preferred the button up collar of her brown dress.

"Angela." Patsy's smile had turned to a frown. "He's waiting."

"Oh yes." Angela had almost forgotten why she was changing her dress.

Their mother bustled in with a bottle of her rose perfume. "A little of this will be all right today." Mother spoke as if she had already had a conversation about the perfume with Angela.

She looked at both her sister and mother and wondered if they were more excited than she. Of course they were, with their romantic hearts.

She stepped into the gently-gathered skirt and pushed her arms through the puffy balloon sleeves. Her mother and sister fluttered around her, fastening the bodice, smoothing her hair.

Then they stopped and stood before her. Both women clasped their hands in front of them and smiled. First to Angela and then to each other.

Patricia gave her another once-over. "She cleans up rather nicely."

"That she does." Her mother nodded and hooked her arm around Angela's elbow. "That nice man is not going to wait forever for you. You better get downstairs."

Angela took a deep breath. Her mother hadn't even given her a moment to check her appearance in her mirror. But as she walked down the steps with all that beautiful fabric swishing around her, she felt beautiful. And nervous. And excited in a way she never had before.

She turned the corner and walked into the parlor. It felt like a dream when she saw Gordon as he stood up, his eyes fixed on her. A hint of a smile curled on his face. He dropped his hat on the settee behind him and strode across the room and reached out to her.

"Miss Harris" He took her hand. "I'm so sorry about the timing. I didn't realize I forgot to put a date on my letter. I hope you'll forgive me."

"Oh, I do. I forgive both you and the post office."

Angela bit her lip, regretting her remark as soon as she spoke it.

With her mother and sister, that would have been funny. But Gordon, his hand shaking, didn't seem to understand as he led her to her chair.

Would the rest of the afternoon be any better? Angela was certain it would be.

Chapter 7
Gordon and Angela

The only thing that could have made the afternoon better would have been sunshine. When Mr. Edwards suggested a stroll down the street so Angela could show him her new surroundings, she wanted to say yes. On a fine day, she would have delighted in a stroll on such a handsome man's arm.

But today, she had to say no, for the weather was forbidding. The wind shook the windows and howled as it passed through the trees in the yard. The sky, iron gray, made the day seem even colder. Patches of ice were all that remained of a gentle snow shower from the previous evening. There was nothing to recommend an outdoor promenade except the company of a gentleman.

Mr. Edwards didn't seem to mind. Instead, he regaled Angela with stories from school. The students who never studied. Those who studied all the time. His lessons. The social gatherings. Angela rarely heard such tales of merriment—she expected college to be a serious pursuit. She suspected Patricia was listening from the kitchen, curious to hear whether a romance was blossoming.

His initial nervousness faded as he relaxed in her presence. So did Angela's own jitters as he laughed more easily and responded to her with a quip or two of his own. He sat back on the settee, comfortable beside her Once he even threw his head back as he chuckled over something she said as she told him about the move to their house and their new friends.

It didn't take long before Mr. Edwards became Gordon and Miss

Harris became Angela.

When her mother invited Gordon to join them for tea, he agreed with alacrity.

He jumped up and offered his arm to Angela. As she accepted his considerate gesture, she began feeling as if they were old friends who had cherished each other for a very long time. Gordon's kindnesses made her feel lighter than she usually did. She couldn't help but smile.

Patricia was already at the table, trying to hold back a grin. Angela had a feeling she and Gordon had been a topic of conversation since his arrival.

"And how are your mother and father, Mr. Edwards?" Patricia failed at her attempt to look nonchalant as she handed him a tray of sandwiches.

"They are very well, thank you."

"How long are you staying in Annapolis, Mr. Edwards?" Mother asked.

"Not long at all. I must get back for a lecture on Wednesday. I came home to see an old friend who has returned from abroad. Then I continued on to see you." He smiled as the blush creeped up his neck.

"Will you be home in time for the Winter Ball, Mr. Edwards? I know I am so looking forward to it." Patricia stirred her tea for the tenth time.

"I expect to be." He looked from Patsy to Angela. "I should be finished my schoolwork so that I can come home for Christmas and the New Year. Mama does insist both my brother John and I attend with her every year. She's quite firm about that."

Patricia picked up her teacup and nodded. "I agree with your mother. You should be there. It's only the best event of the winter season."

"I would certainly hope to find both you and your sister willing to join me for a dance," he said to Patricia. "I enjoy dancing but don't get to many parties, I'm afraid."

"But you talked about the parties at school—" Patricia blushed as she realized she had been caught eavesdropping.

Although Angela glared at her sister, Gordon laughed. "So I did. And you heard all about it, did you? My apologies for not inviting you in to join our conversation."

Patricia's blush grew deeper. "I didn't mean…"

"I know you didn't. And you are correct, Miss Patricia. I have taken part in a number of social engagements while at William and Mary. It's almost a requirement. But only a few of them require dancing."

The exchange between her friend and her sister charmed Angela. How graciously he ribbed Patsy for eavesdropping and then spoke so kindly to her. She knew in the presence of some other men this could have been an embarrassing moment. Her affection for Gordon grew stronger every moment.

She caught his eye when he passed the cream and he smiled at her.

"As for the ball, I will do my best to arrange my plans to be home by then. It is, as you said, Miss Patricia, a wonderful affair. I expect you will have dozens of suitors seeking you out."

Patricia sighed loudly and shook her head. "My beau, the only man I wish to dance with, will be elsewhere that evening."

"Oh? I'm so sorry to hear that." Gordon cocked his head as if waiting for the rest of her answer.

Angela wanted to laugh. He seemed to understand her sister's dramatic ways.

"Yes, his mother insisted they spend the winter at her family home in Frederick. He's been there for weeks already. I miss him."

Patricia grew silent as a dark look passed over her face.

"I'm sure he misses you as well, Miss Patricia." Gordon looked at her with a sympathetic smile.

"Do you think so?" Patricia looked at him with such hope. "I was beginning to wonder."

"Of course he does, dear," Mother answered. "Now cheer up. You're upsetting our guest and we don't want him to go away thinking we are the saddest people in the world."

"Madam, I could never think that." A hint of pink tinged his pale cheek. "I am grateful for your hospitality."

After tea concluded, Patsy and Mother retreated upstairs to allow

Angela and Gordon a few last moments alone.

"I really would be delighted to join you at the ball. Both you and your sister of course."

"I'd love it," Angela said simply.

"I, that is to say," Gordon stammered, "I hope you'll…"

Angela thought she knew what he wanted to say. Even though she dare not say it, it was what she wanted, too. "I'm looking forward to spending the evening with you."

Gordon exhaled and smiled at her. "Miss…Angela…There is something I should tell you. Those social engagements at college, well, we meet all the local ladies. And sometimes, well…"

Angela stopped and looked at him, anxious for him to continue.

"Well, I befriended one young lady but I never stop thinking of you."

Even though she didn't know exactly what he meant by "befriended," Angela wanted to give him the benefit of the doubt. That's what friends did, didn't they?

She smiled kindly as she answered. "That is something you prove with every letter. Of course you've met the ladies in Williamsburg. But I am delighted you continue our correspondence. It does me good to receive your letters. I hope you feel the same."

"Yes, I do. Every single one warms my heart. But—"

"Oh, Mr. Edwards. We have no understanding." Angela blushed at her own directness. But it needed to be said. "I expect you have many friends. I am glad to be counted among them."

"Yes, I'm glad I told you then." He looked at his pocket watch, a big gold thing hanging from a heavy chain. "I'm afraid I have overstayed my welcome. Mama is expecting me home."

He offered her his arm as they walked to the door. She liked the closeness, the spicy smell of his fine dark wool coat, the firm arm underneath that sleeve. He took her hand before leaving and kissed it ever so sweetly. As he did, Angela wondered with a frisson of jealousy, if that other young lady received such attentions. She was surprised at herself, wishing they were reserved for her alone.

"Thank you for a wonderful afternoon." Gordon bowed and put on his hat before leaving.

As he turned down the street and out of sight, Angela caught a whiff of Gordon's warm scent on her own skin. It made her close her eyes and sigh. She returned to the parlor and the glint of something on the settee caught her attention. A little gold key with Greek letters was lodged between the cushions.

Since she didn't recognize it, she figured it must belong to Gordon. She tucked it in her pocket and caressed it with her fingers. Such a fine little charm, she knew he would miss it. She must write to him so he could reclaim it.

As she reached the top of the stairs, Patsy peeked out from her mother's chamber. Angela could see she wasn't about to get away without further comment from her sister.

"Gordon's gone?" Patsy wore a look of sheer innocence on her face.

"You know he is. And you probably heard everything he said since tea." She followed her sister in to talk to Mother.

Patricia made a face. "Not from up here. Sometimes the two of you were mumbling so I couldn't hear anything at all."

Angela laughed. "Let me think. What did you miss?" As she took a chair by the fire, she put her hand in her pocket and felt the cold metal of Gordon's charm beside his most recent letter. Yes, she would write about the errant key as soon as she spoke with Mother.

"So tell me about the ball." Patricia was relentless.

"Patsy," her mother interjected. "Give your sister a moment."

"Thank you, Mother." Angela's thoughts were a jumble. She was so surprised and pleased by Gordon's kindness and his affection. Mixed in with those pleasures was his comment about another lady friend. It was a warning perhaps. A sign to keep her head firmly on her shoulders? She must remain sensible about her friendship with him.

"He's quite a delightful young man," Mother said in the silence that followed.

Angela nodded. "We had a wonderful visit." She didn't want to say more, didn't know what to say. Being the subject of a gentleman's attentions felt so strange and glorious to Angela. She didn't know how to act.

"What about the ball?" Patsy repeated.

"Oh yes. You know everything I know. Gordon plans to attend. He will attend with his parents and brother. He has asked that you reserve a dance for him."

Patsy clapped her hands. "Then he means to spend the evening dancing with you."

Angela couldn't help the heat rising up to her cheeks. "I would never presume such a thing. After all, there will be other ladies. Including his mother."

"What about his friend in Williamsburg? Perhaps she'll be there."

Oh yes, Patsy would remember the only slightly uncomfortable moment of the day, the one thing Angela didn't want to talk about. "You did hear quite a lot, didn't you, Patsy?"

"I only wish I did. But I wasn't sure who he was talking about. I told you I couldn't hear everything."

"He merely meant he has an acquaintance in town."

"And you aren't worried? Suspicious? Jealous? If Vincent told me about some acquaintance in Frederick, I think it would break my heart."

"The difference, Patsy, is you have an understanding with Vincent."

Patsy's face fell at her sister's comment.

"Don't you?" Angela had been sure their relationship had become serious. There had been no mention of an engagement but surely that was imminent.

"No, not in so many words." Patsy's lower lip quivered. "He's said many lovely things to me but never once has he told me he loved me."

Their mother put her needlework down. "Do you mean to tell me after all this time, Vincent has made no declaration of love? I presumed you two were talking about marriage."

"I wish we were," Patsy sighed. "He only promised we'd be together soon after the New Year."

"Well that's something," Mother picked up her needle. "Even though I was hoping for a spring wedding."

"So was I." Patricia's voice was wistful. "How did we start talking about Vincent? We were talking about Mr. Edwards and his friend in Williamsburg.”

“I don’t think you need to worry about Mr. Edwards’s friend.”

Patricia opened her little volume of poetry. “No, I don’t but I think you do.”

Chapter 8
Only Dinner

"Patsy, you'll need to set another place at the table." Mother adjusted the forks beside Uncle Max's plate and eyed the flatware as Patsy laid it down.

"Who's coming to dinner? We haven't had company in ages." She reached into the knife case for the additional cutlery.

"Max invited Mr. Taylor."

Her momentary excitement deflated. "Oh. That's nice."

Uncle Max had teased her the previous night about Mr. Taylor's interest in her. "Ah yes. He asks me about Miss Patricia every day," he had said.

Patsy immediately mentioned her recent letter to Vincent. It was enough to cut the conversation short. If only temporarily. Now as she laid the silver, she had a feeling her uncle was plotting something.

The attentions from Mr. Taylor were flattering, if unwelcome. He was a very nice man, but since he had to be well into his twenties—maybe even thirty—he was much too old for her.

Not only that, Patsy couldn't bear even the slightest trace of disloyalty to Vincent. If only he would write to her as he promised. Frederick must be an exciting place to keep Vincent from his writing desk.

"Hello, Miss Patricia." Mr. Taylor greeted her with warm brown eyes and a smile that put a dimple in his cheek. He did have such a kind face and a deep musical voice. If only he weren't so old. If only he were Vincent.

"Mr. Taylor. Mother just told me you would be here for the noon meal. I'm delighted to see you again."

"May I help you?"

"What a thing to ask, sir! Indeed you may not. Uncle Max is waiting for you in the parlor."

"Yes, it was he who suggested I come say hello." Even though Mr. Taylor was surely too old to blush, he did it anyway.

Patricia simply didn't know how to react. The tinge in his cheeks made him look almost boyish. She laid down the last of the spoons. "Well, I'm glad you did. Miss Ella said dinner will be ready shortly."

"It does smell delicious."

"It's only oyster stew."

"Wonderful. That's my favorite."

"Miss Ella makes the best I've ever had."

"That's very good news, indeed."

Patricia couldn't figure out how to convince Mr. Taylor to return to the parlor. She was uncomfortable at his nearness. Encouraging his attentions, she believed, was to be unfaithful to Vincent. That was something she couldn't do. And yet, Mr. Taylor was so kind, so attentive.

She shooed him from the dining room only to have him take up the chair next to hers when the meal was called.

He included her in everything he said, whether it was a comment about the weather or a remark about politics. He turned to her again and again with a smile or a nod.

Mr. Taylor ate heartily, she noticed, polishing off a second bowl of the stew with relish. "Thank you for such a delightful dinner, Mrs. Harris," he said. "Your daughter assured me your cook made outstanding stew."

Mother's face lit up at the praise. "That's very kind of you to say, William. I'll be sure to tell Ella."

He pushed his chair from the table and laid his napkin beside his plate. "If you'll excuse me, I have an appointment shortly. I thank you again for such a delicious repast but I really must go. It will be a busy afternoon."

William moved to take his leave. "Miss Patricia, I look forward to seeing you again tomorrow." With that gesture, he bowed and left.

"I'll be in the shop in a little while," Max shouted to William's retreating back.

"What did he mean he'd see me tomorrow?" Patsy asked.

Max ladled another serving of the creamy stew. "What? Oh, I told him he could come by every noontime. We always have plenty and Will, poor man, needs a family to look after him."

The news sent shivers through Patsy. "So he'll be here every day?"

She appreciated her uncle's generous gesture. She was pleased by Mr. Taylor's attentions. But she felt a little guilty, too. She had to stay true to Vincent. Or was the lack of communication from him a sign that it was permissible to accept the attentions of Mr. Taylor. Her feelings were in quite a muddle.

"How lovely." Angela slid mischievous eyes toward Patsy as she picked up her wine glass.

Patricia, still uneasy about Vincent and Mr. Taylor, arranged her escape the following day when a morning visit with Jane included an invitation to stay for dinner. Even if she couldn't stay away every day, she was determined to find excuses when she could.

Arriving home in mid-afternoon, she found Angela at her secretary, going through the day's mail. She handed Patsy a thin red leather-bound volume of poetry.

"Mr. Taylor left this for you. He had hoped you would read to him. He told me it was from his own collection. I think he was disappointed when you weren't here."

"Don't think you can make me feel guilty, Miss Angela." That was, however, exactly how Patricia felt as she leafed through the pages of the small dusty volume. "It is a thoughtful gift, isn't it? I'll be sure to thank him tomorrow."

Angela looked up from the letter in her hand. Patricia could see she meant to be kind. "He really does care, you know. His attentions are directed almost exclusively to you. Mother and I are merely chaperons."

"Oh don't say that. I can't possibly fall in love with Mr. Taylor. For one thing, he's so old."

"Old!" Angela exclaimed. "How can you say that?"

"He fought in the war with Uncle Max. That was twenty years ago."

Angela smiled. "He was a drummer boy. While it is true that Mr. Taylor served during the Battle of Baltimore, he carried only a drum, never a gun. Uncle Max heard him telling everyone he was sixteen but found out later Mr. Taylor was only twelve. He'd run away from the orphanage to join the army. After the war ended, Uncle Max took him under his wing as a sort of father figure. That was in 1814."

Patricia tried to figure out his age but before coming up with an answer Angela replied. "He's twenty-nine."

"Oh. Well, must I remind you? I've already given my heart to my dear Vincent."

"Sweetheart, your Vincent may not be yours at all."

Patricia recoiled as if Angela had struck her cheek. "No. Please don't say that. He will write. I know he will. The minute he's able he'll send me one of his tender letters. I must remain steadfast in my love for him. You have to understand that."

Angela nodded and looked back at her correspondence. "For your sake, for your heart's sake, I hope you're right. But for Mr. Taylor's sake, I hope you'll at least be kind to him."

Patricia settled in a chair by the window with her new book of poetry. "Of course, I'll be kind to him. But that is all I will be: kind to an old friend of Uncle Max."

Mother swept into the room as Patricia finished speaking. "You're speaking of Mr. Taylor? You know he isn't that old."

Patricia nodded. "Yes, Angela just explained that to me. She told me all about his service during the Battle of Baltimore."

"That's where your Uncle Max met Mr. Taylor. ." Mother sat on the settee with that look in her eye, the one that warned Patricia she was going to be on the receiving end of her mother's lectures. Never stern, always gentle, they were designed to make her think sensibly. As if she didn't do that already.

"Mother, he's nearly thirty. I'm only eighteen. He's eleven years old than me."

"Yes and what does that prove? Your father was twice my age. He was well established and able to provide a very good life for all of us. We had a happy marriage. He was a good man, always kind to me. I miss him every day."

When she looked as if she might sob, both daughters rushed to her, Angela at her knee and Patricia by her elbow. "We all do, Mother." Angela whispered as she reached out her hands to her mother and sister. "It isn't the same without him."

Though her eyes shone with tears she held back, their mother smiled at both daughters. "At least I have the two of you."

"And you always shall," Angela said as Patricia nodded.

Maybe her mother had a point, but she still couldn't compare the handsome, young Vincent with Mr. Taylor. And she didn't want to.

When she set the table for dinner the following day, she remembered to set a place for him.

And when he arrived, she greeted him as brightly as she could. "Good afternoon."

"Miss Patricia, how good to see you today." Mr. Taylor's gaze held hers as they took their places.

Her unsteady heart skipped a beat and she had to look away. "I'm sorry I missed seeing you yesterday. I was visiting with Jane." Then she remembered the book of verses. "I must thank you for the little volume of poetry. I don't know if I've ever read Coleridge before."

"I find his work far different from earlier English poets. There's a poem called 'Love' in the book that tells of a knight and his lady. I thought you might appreciate that one." He blushed.

Patricia couldn't believe her eyes. This was the second time she'd seen him blush like a schoolboy. The fact that he blushed about a poem made at her consider him a little differently as she passed him the platter of ham. "I'll look it up right after dinner."

And she meant it. To her way of thinking there was nothing so fine as a poem of lords and ladies. They were the characters of a far different time and place, very unlike her mundane surroundings in Annapolis.

"Perhaps we could read it together. I have a little more time to spare today." Mr. Taylor looked upon her with soft eyes, pleading much as her pup did. How could she say no?

LOVE LETTERS & GINGERBREAD

"Splendid idea." Patricia tucked into her dinner, suddenly realizing she looked forward to reading with him. Mr. Taylor was a surprise. She shot him sidelong glances as he picked up the thread of conversation with Uncle Max and Mother.

Twenty-nine was still old. And yet she was beginning to think maybe she should reassess her feelings for him—if only because of his fine taste in poetry. At the very least, it would make their noontime meals more enjoyable.

A message came for Uncle Max as the meal neared its conclusion. He frowned as he read it, then smiled. "William. Carson has agreed to meet with us to go over our proposal. I'm afraid, dear ladies, we will have to cut short our time today. We've been negotiating with this shipper for what seems like months. Can't keep him waiting now. We must go right away."

"Yes, of course, sir." Mr. Taylor stood as he prepared to depart with Max. First, he turned to Patricia, the disappointment apparent in his expression. "I realize this means I cannot stay and read with you today. Perhaps tomorrow?" He stopped and thought. "No, I can't tomorrow. Another time, then."

Patricia's heart went out to him as he gazed into her eyes. "I will save the Love poem for when we are together again."

"Oh no, Miss Patricia. I wouldn't ask that of you. I think you will enjoy it. You can tell me what you think tomorrow. No, not tomorrow. The next time I'm here."

He took her hand and pressed his lips to it. Such a gentlemanly gesture, it made Patricia's heart skip a beat as she whispered her response. "Yes, I will. I promise. Thank you."

He bowed and the two men were gone, leaving the three ladies alone at the table.

"My dear daughter. William is quite smitten." A look of delight shone in Mother's eyes.

"I'm not sure he really heard a word anyone of us said. You captured all his attention." Angela nibbled at the last of her bread.

"I didn't mean to." She was flattered. She couldn't help but be. Mr. Taylor was doing this utmost to please her. As charming as Vincent always was, he never went out of his way to make her happy as Mr.

Taylor seemed bent on doing. In recent weeks, he couldn't even manage write and post a letter.

"It doesn't matter what you meant to do, it seems Mr. Taylor is determined to win your heart." Her mother led the way to the parlor. "We must start thinking about the gingerbread."

"Gingerbread?" Angela clapped her hands. "I love baking gingerbread. Do you think Miss Ella will be able to help us?"

"I know she will." Her mother sat in the chair by the window to mend a torn skirt hem. "She told me she's quite knowledgeable in the ways of German cooking."

"And a Tannenbaum, too?" Patsy loved the tradition of a decorated fir tree.

"Of course. Uncle Max and I spoke about that a few days ago."

Patricia glanced at the little book of verses she promised to read. It would have to wait. If her mother and sister were going to discuss Christmas preparations, she wanted to be in on the conversation. Last year's Christmas, she recalled with an ache, had been so sad and dreary. This year would have to be much happier. Their futures, though not secure, were more settled this season. It appeared her sister might have a beau—although it was so hard to tell with Angela. She talked about him only rarely and Patsy suspected she had never even made her affections clear to him. Two such reserved people trying to fall in love could test the patience.

And what did she have to look forward to herself? Though Vincent seemed to have disappeared from her life, he was never far from her thoughts. Mr. Taylor…he might be endearing but Patricia wasn't sure how she could transfer her feelings from her one true love to a kind older man. Her mother thought it a splendid match. The best she could say was she was glad he liked poetry. Maybe that was a start.

"Patricia, see if you can find my receipts. They should be in the bottom drawer of the chiffonier."

As Patricia went into the kitchen, she imagined she could already smell the heavy spice of Christmas. This year's holiday, no matter how her heart might ache, would be much happier than last year's.

Chapter 9
The value of letters

Angela couldn't keep from feeling lonely. Even though she was trying her hardest to be bright and cheerful, she felt so alone. Of course she was glad for Patsy. Her sister's heart had clearly softened for William. Thrown together every mid-day, they had turned into a sort of a pair. She couldn't help feeling like the odd one out as she laughed along with them and kept up her end of the conversation.

She never felt sorry for herself. Not exactly.

But could Angela help it as she passed the serving platter if she wished it was Gordon rather than Uncle Max at her side? If it was Gordon's eyes she longed to gaze into? His hand she accidentally brushed against when she refilled his glass?

Instead, she put her hand inside her pocket and found comfort in the smooth paper with its sharp corners resting there, waiting for her. She always kept Gordon's latest letter within reach. This one was new, still unopened as the morning's duties had kept her away from it. She longed to read it and would, as soon as the noon meal concluded.

These little notes, usually short and, judging from the ill-formed letters and occasional ink smears, written quickly, were so valuable to Angela. Every single day, one of Gordon's letters was always safe in the pocket of her dress.

After dinner, when she was at last alone, she took her usual seat by the secretary, took out the latest letter and ran her cool fingers over the dog-eared note.

She loved how he formed the initials in her name. The long strokes and curved sweep at the beginning of the A and the crossbar of the H signaled to her Gordon's sweet regard.

By contrast, the scribbled lines inside ran uphill. This letter had fewer blotches than the last but an ink smear swept across the bottom edge of the sheet. None of that was important.

Only the message mattered:

"My workload has not been insignificant this past week. So much reading! So much writing! But I quickly put it aside when a letter from you, Dear Angela, arrives in the afternoon mail. Your words ease my burdens every time you write."

Angela re-read the sentences. "Dear Angela" made her sigh. She was glad to be of aid to this dear man. It was good to be useful. She wondered if perhaps he meant more than those words of appreciation. He was so busy and yet he took out time for her. Even if the letter was written hurriedly, he sat down, thought of her and wrote.

Much as she delighted in her new friend Gordon, she didn't dare imagine life as his spouse. He had never intimated in any way that he was considering a future together with her. And, for her part, she couldn't imagine leaving her mother alone, not after this past painful year. His friendship would have to be enough. That was the sensible position to take, but as she folded the prized page she knew mere friendship would never be enough.

She missed him, she thought as she slipped it into her pocket. There it would remain until his next letter arrived. Angela saved them all, making room in one of the slots in her desk, beside the other important papers. It was nearly full now. She counted on his letters nearly as much as he said he relied on hers.

The narrow slot jam-packed with his thoughts, his news and his sweet words of affection soothed her loneliness. She prized them all, becoming more certain that her feelings toward Gordon were growing stronger everyday.

Angela was counting the days until he returned home for the Winter Ball. She hadn't looked forward to the annual gathering like this since she was Patsy's age, attending for the first time. She remembered how her mother had fussed over her dress, a creamy confection with thick lace dripping from the scooped neck, the puffed sleeves, the hem of the narrow bell of the under dress. The gauzy overdress was trimmed in spangles and gold thread that sparkled in the candlelight.

She danced and danced that night. She should have felt beautiful but, as an awkward and shy teenager, she could barely hold up her end of a conversation. She pasted on her best smile with each new partner. Alas, she made no memorable impression on any of the young men she met.

Afterwards, there were no suitors. No offers of marriage. She sat home and waited, hopeful someone would call. Even if she couldn't remember a single gentleman's name.

When no one came, she declared herself unmarriageable and resigned herself to a life of helping her family.

Her father must have seen the sadness in her eyes. He asked for her help in his busy physician's practice. It was there she gained much needed confidence as she met new people. She discovered her interest in medicine, in numbers and record-keeping. She pushed her shyness away to speak not only to sick little children and their worried parents but to haughty physicians who thought they could dismiss her even though she determined who would—and who would not—call on her father.

Now she was glad to be able to serve as a helper to her dear mother, still recovering from her loss. When Mother couldn't face her days without her husband, Angela had quietly taken over paying the bills, answering the correspondence, overseeing their move to Uncle Max's. Mother was happy to let most of these tasks remain hers even after she rose from mourning.

Although Patsy needed her more than ever, as she navigated the new world of womanhood, Angela was often at a loss as to how to help. She feared Vincent was breaking her little sister's heart. Much as they all loved him, his silence was painful.

Angela and her mother held their breath every time the mail came, hoping that this would be the day Vincent wrote.

Angela even felt a little guilty when another letter arrived for her but none came for Patsy. She tried to spare her sister's feelings, taking the letter without comment, reading it only when she was alone. She never discussed the contents of Gordon's notes, nor her growing attachment to him. She couldn't let her own new feelings distress Patsy further.

Instead, Angela and her mother did everything they could think of to soothe Patsy's pain. Invitations to tea were sent to Jane. Outings were planned when the weather was fine. Uncle Max made a horse and carriage available. They even scheduled their gingerbread making day for far earlier than they should have, hoping to keep Patsy's spirits up.

Uncle Max took their ministrations a step further when he invited William to share their noon meals. He never said a word about his motives but both Angela and Mother—and probably Patsy, too—had their suspicions.

Maybe it helped. It seemed Patsy was learning to care for William but even so, she still . continued to wait for letters that never came.

The following day was shopping day. There were so many things to buy before cookie baking could commence. Angela and Patsy chattered nonstop as they accompanied Mother and Ella to the crowded shops for the precious spices, sugar and flour, butter and eggs.

The cookie molds and cutters, handed down from Mother's grandmother who emigrated from Germany, were already unpacked, washed and rubbed dry, waiting for the next day's activities.

They returned home with their nostrils filled with the warm fragrances of nutmeg and ginger. Their arms ached from the heavy bags of flour.

"I am starving." Patsy heaved her packages onto the smooth, worn kitchen table. "All I want are walnuts. May I, Mother?" Patsy was already digging through the drawer for the nutcracker before her mother could answer.

"Make sure you save some for Christmas, Miss Patricia." Miss Ella's voice was stern but Patricia saw the warmth in her eyes.

"Of course, Miss Ella. I only want a couple. Anybody else want some?" While Mother and Miss Ella unpacked their purchases, Patricia cracked open two plump brown walnuts. Their woodsy scent filled the air and made Patricia's mouth water. They were her favorite and it was only in December that she could get her fill.

The first was so sweet with the right amount of crunch. She savored the feel of the nut's smooth brown ridges on her tongue and chewed slowly. As she cracked the second one, anxiously awaiting it as she had the first, Angela placed a bundle tied with a rough brown twine on the table in front of her.

"Angela, can't you see I'm using this spot?" She pushed the papers away, giving them no heed at first. Then something about them caught her eye. The handwriting was familiar. The name and Frederick address she knew as well as her own.

Patricia didn't want the second walnut after all. "Where did these come from?" Her voice was small. She really didn't want to hear the answer.

"They were with the morning mail. I was just going through it— oh Patsy, I'm so sorry. There was a note: 'Return to sender.' "

Patricia didn't like the pity she saw in her sister's expression. No, this couldn't be right. There had to be a mistake.

Maybe she wrote the address incorrectly. No, they matched the address he had given her. Perhaps the post office delivered them to the wrong house. She hoped that was it. She couldn't imagine that Vincent would refuse and send back every single letter she sent.

She ripped off the string and rifled through the letters. She'd lost count of how many she sent. So she didn't know if this was all of them. There was such a lot of them it had to be the whole complement. She held back tears—no, she wasn't going to cry—as she saw her notes had gone unopened, unheeded, unwanted.

She started to put them down when a tiny card separated from the stack. Gasping, she quickly scanned it.

"Return to sender. Addressee unknown."

The kitchen was quiet as a church. Mother lay a hand on her daughter's shoulder as Ella slipped silently from the room. Not even Angela spoke.

Patricia could hear her heart pound and listened to find out if it would sound differently now that it was breaking. She didn't want to believe Vincent refused her letters. She preferred to think this was all a terrible error or misunderstanding.

The letters seemed to taunt her. What a fool she had been, giving her heart to him.

Mother broke the pain-filled quiet. "But he promised…"

"I wish he had, Mother." What a fool she was, trusting he loved her, too. "But all he said was he would see me after the new year. I guess he changed his mind."

"But surely—" Mother's lip quivered. Dear Mother was swept up in his charm too.

Patricia could only shake her head. What a fool she was, believing he would think only of her while they were apart.

"My dear Patsy." It was when her mother encircled Patricia in a loving embrace that the sobs came, soft but strong, from deep within her soul.

She leaned her cheek against her mother's shoulder. "I've been a fool, Mother."

"No, my sweet girl, you've been a loving, trusting soul. I wouldn't expect anything less from you. It's how God made you, full of heart."

Patricia wanted the words to make her feel better. She wanted to believe her emotions hadn't gotten the best of her. She wanted for the first time in her life to be cool the way Angela was cool. Her sister stood there, her hand in her pocket, unperturbed by the torture inflicted on Patricia by those odious letters.

She hid her wet face in her mother's warmth letting what comfort she could get soothe her. Her stomach ached and her heart felt like it had stopped beating.

"Come, my dear Patsy." Mother held out her crumpled handkerchief. "Dry your face."

Patricia looked up to see tears welling in her mother's eyes. Oh that Vincent! He had hurt her mother, too. Big, loud sobs wracked her body as she took refuge again in her mother's soft arms.

Angela put the kettle on for tea. That was so like her. All the world was falling apart and she had to take care of household things. Just as well. A cup of tea might hold body and soul together.

Chapter 10
Gingerbread

The kitchen smelled of ginger, cloves and nutmeg. Patricia breathed in the aromas of Christmas as her sister and mother bent over a hot pan of gingerbread, trying to ascertain whether it was fully baked.

Ella glanced at the pan with a knowing look and nodded. "Oh it's done, Miss Olivia."

"It's been so long since I've baked these." Mother eyed the golden brown edges. "It's a wonder Max suggested it."

"I made them at my last house, before I bought my freedom," Ella eased the pan from Mother's hands and laid it down to cool. "The people there liked the old German traditions, too. So I learned how to make gingerbread and stollen and a couple of other recipes with long German names."

Patricia lounged in a corner, absent-mindedly patting Timmy who was fast asleep in her lap while she read from her favorite book of poetry. Much as she loved gingerbread, she had little interest in baking it. She'd taken refuge in the kitchen because it was warm and cozy on a blustery winter day.

"Oh, do listen to this." The poetic words, so often a comfort, seemed to have lost their lustre today but she hoped reading them would cheer her up for such a festive occasion. "It's beautiful."

She sat up, cleared her throat in a dainty fashion and held her book out to read: *One sweet thing there is still, that from within, Within us speaks—that may be felt afar; This may be wafted o'er to thee alone.*

"Isn't that beautiful? It's from Goethe's 'The Christmas Box.'"

"Gorgeous, Patsy. But whatever does that mean?" Mother asked without taking her eyes off the cookies.

"Do you know what's beautiful?" Angela put her hand on her hip.

"What?" Patsy looked up dreamily from her dog and her poems.

"A young lady who helps her mother. That's something beautiful." Count on Angela to be practical, not even slightly mindful of Patsy's aching heart. At least she could rely on her dog to stay close and soothe her pain.

"How true." Patsy smiled in spite of her sister's chiding. "It looks very becoming on you."

"Girls!" Mother intervened. "We'll never get the gingerbread done if you pester one another. Angela, get that other baking sheet ready. Ella's almost ready for it. And you, Miss Poetry, put down your pup and find your apron. We need your help."

With a frown, Patricia slid a pale blue ribbon in her book and closed it. As she reached for her apron, there was a knock at the front door. Timmy raced to the front of the house, Patricia apparently forgotten.

"Uncle Max has answered the door. Oh, it's Jane," she announced after looking after the disappearing dog. "She's with another girl. I don't recognize her."

"She told us her cousin Kitty was coming," Mother recalled.

Uncle Max led the girls into the kitchen.

"Look who I found standing on our doorstep." Max smiled at them and turned to his sister. "You just said you needed more help, Olivia."

"Oh, it smells so good in here!" Jane breathed in the spicy fragrance. "Hello, Mrs. Harris. Hello, Angela. Patricia. This is Kitty Baxter, my cousin who is visiting from Virginia." Then she smiled. "It looked like we picked a very good time to visit indeed."

"Whatever is that smell?" Angela noticed the new girl's southern drawl right away. A pretty girl, she had sparkling blue eyes, dimples in her rounded cheeks and clusters of black curls around her face.

"Gingerbread," Mother answered. "We're making decorations for the *Tannenbaum*. The Christmas tree."

The girl looked puzzled. "What? I've never heard of such a thing."

"Oh it's a German tradition," Angela answered as she offered each of the girls a warm, molded cookie, redolent in exotic spices that always made her think of the holiday. Uncle Max had been biding his time and gladly took one before he sat on a stool beside the table.

"Mmmm," Jane said after she took a bite. "You are going to hang these on a tree?" She looked out the window and turned back looking even more puzzled.

"Well, yes, but not one of the trees outside." Mother laughed. "We will cut down a little fir tree. Max already has one picked out, don't you?"

He nodded. "I found one this summer when I was walking through the woods. I have kept my eye on it."

"And then what do you do with it?" Kitty asked.

"On Christmas Eve, we'll place it on a table in the parlor and decorate it with apples and nuts, this gingerbread and candles. To welcome the *Christkind*."

"What a lovely tradition." Kitty's eyes were wide in wonder. "Mmmmm. What's a *Christkind*?"

"That's the Baby Jesus," Patsy wondered if the girl knew anything at all. Or maybe these were traditions she didn't keep down South. "Our grandparents came from Germany and Uncle Max and Mother like to remember the old Christmas traditions."

"This one anyway." Angela thought for a moment her mother was going to cry. She hadn't been sad in so long but Angela knew her mother might be feeling a little wistful without Father this year.

Then Mother smiled. "You'll have to come over on Christmas Eve to see the tree all lit up."

"And then we sing *Stille Nacht*. That's 'Silent Night'—do you know the Christmas song?" Angela asked. "Mother, you have to sing it."

"Oh no," Mother demurred. "You girls can sing the song. I don't have much of a voice these days."

Patsy hummed the gentle tune for a moment and then sang the words in German: "*Stille nacht, heilige nacht.*"

Ella joined in on the second line, singing the German lines in a rich throaty alto voice. Patsy stopped to listen to her as she finished the first stanza.

The room grew silent as the last strains of the verse faded away. Ella looked around the room. "Well, aren't you going to sing?"

Angela joined in for the second German stanza and then nodded to Patsy and Ella and they finished in English, "Sleep in heavenly peace."

"Such a pretty song," Jane clapped her hands. "I never heard it before."

"That did sound lovely." Uncle Max nodded as he popped the last bit of cookie in his mouth. "And your cookies? Those are splendid, too.

Angela jumped up to help Ella retrieve the next batch of cookies from the oven. "We still have a little more baking to do," She turned to their visitors. "Would you like to help?"

"I would!" Jane pulled off her bonnet. "Kitty?"

Kitty folded her hands and moved away from the bowls and pans and gingerbread mold. "I really ought to get back and unpack," she smiled. "The minute I arrived Jane took my hand and told me I must meet the Harris girls."

"I was sure Kitty would like meeting other girls our age," Jane added.

"I do hope you won't mind if I turn down your kind offer." Kitty looked most apologetic. "I do look forward to seeing your Christmas bush."

Uncle Max laughed and rose to put an arm around the girl. "And so you shall. It will be a beautiful bush." He looked back at his nieces and cocked an eyebrow before leading her down the hall. "That's more than a week away, though. I hope you'll come to visit before then."

Kitty popped back in the kitchen. "I almost forgot my manners. It was a pleasure to meet all of you. Goodbye."

As soon as the door closed, Patricia sat down at the kitchen table across from Jane. Her apron remained on its hook.

"What do you think of her?" Jane asked.

Mother joined the girls at the table. "She seems like a lovely girl. Such a beautiful accent. Where did you say she is from?"

"Williamsburg."

Angela started at Jane's answer. She wondered if perhaps this girl met Gordon at one of his social engagements. Much as she wanted to put the idea out of her mind, she also wanted to know more. She sat down at the table.

"I haven't seen my cousin in several years," Jane added. "The last time she was here, she tore her dress, had mud on her face and couldn't keep her shoes tied. She's turned into a quite a lady. A Southern belle. And those clothes. I'm envious."

Patsy giggled. "Jane, I didn't think there was an evil bone in your body."

"Turns out there is," Jane answered frankly. "At least when it comes to Kitty. She waltzed into the house like she was the Queen of Sheba. She told me on the walk over here she's already engaged to a boy from around here. She's only sixteen! I think she said his name is Gregory. Or was it Grover? She said their engagement hasn't been announced yet. Even her mother doesn't know yet."

Angela only half listened to Jane's comments until she mentioned a boy whose name began with G. Then she sat up to hear the rest.

"Then why on earth are you telling us?" Mother asked.

"No good comes from gossip," Ella shook her head as she took another baking pan out of the oven. "If I was listening to all that gossip, these would have been burned."

Angela and her mother jumped up to help transfer the cookies. "Glad you were here, then." Mother laughed. "They do smell wonderful."

While she and her mother inspected the cookies, Jane bent toward Patsy and whispered something Angela couldn't hear. She didn't know whether she wanted to hear the rest of the conversation or get away. Jane's confidences troubled her even though she didn't believe Kitty could be acquainted with Gordon.

Once the cookies were baked, she excused herself from the hot kitchen. The walk to her bedchamber cooled her flushed cheeks but did nothing to ease her alarm. She picked up the lace-edged handkerchief tucked in the dressing table drawer. She unfolded it to reveal Gordon's tiny gold charm.

When she found it on the settee, she thought it was good luck—a sign Gordon would return to fetch it and to see her. Now she wondered if it was only a remembrance of a man who could not be hers. She felt tears welling in her eyes but instead of crying, she laughed at herself.

"Look at me," she said to the reflection in her mirror. "I'm turning into a romantic every bit as silly as Patsy."

She looked at the key for one more moment before folding up the handkerchief and returning it to its place in the drawer.

She was being silly, she told herself again. Then she smoothed back the curly tendrils and calmly walked down to the kitchen. There was still too much baking to finish this afternoon. Moping about wouldn't change anything.

CHAPTER 11
KITTY'S PLAN

Angela was looking out the window when Kitty sidled up to her. Lost in her thoughts, she was startled by the sound of her visitor's voice. She had, after all, slipped away to escape all the excited chatter of her sister and friends as they picked out hair ribbons to wear the following night.

For the past three days, the Winter Ball was all the girls talked about. Angela and Patsy had chosen their dresses and mended their gloves.

This afternoon, Jane and Kitty arrived right after dinner. Jane brought a basket filled with hair ribbons while Kitty chattered endlessly about the ball which she expected to be so much grander than any of the parties she attended in Williamsburg.

Angela had only half-listened while Kitty talked about learning the steps of the gavotte and proclaimed it the most delightful of dances. They discussed their clothes, shoes, clothes and wraps in excruciating detail. It reached the point where she didn't think she could endure another discussion of dancing shoes, fans or how best to tie a sash.

Her heart was full of its own excitement. Gordon would be home tomorrow. How she missed him.

Finally, she sought refuge in the quiet parlor, away from the gaiety.

When Kitty followed her down, Angela could think of no good excuse to refuse her so she patted the cushion and bid her to join her on the settee.

"I've so enjoyed our visit today," Kitty began with a simpering smile.

"We spend a lot of time by ourselves in this house. It's always nice to have visitors." Angela hoped her answer wasn't too rude. If it was, Kitty didn't seem to notice.

"I have been looking forward to meeting you. We have an acquaintance in common, I do believe."

"Yes? I don't think I know anyone in Virginia." Angela didn't want to confide in this girl at all.

"Aren't you acquainted with Mr. Edwards? He's reading the law at the College of William and Mary. I'm sure he told me the two of you met recently." Kitty's eyes were wide with curiosity. Angela wasn't sure, however, that the girl's innocent expression was, actually, innocent. She knew she must think quickly.

"Yes, of course." Angela turned on her smile, as if she suddenly remembered. "He lives on the other side of town but we have, in fact, been introduced."

"Introduced? Now, Angela, I believe it's much more than that."

Angela couldn't imagine where this was leading. She stood up and walked across the room to get away from the brightness of the girl's stare.

"Mr. Edwards tells me you have been acquainted for several months. In fact, he said he came here on his last visit home."

Angela didn't like getting caught in a lie. But even worse, she disliked the line of questioning from this girl, practically a stranger. She had no intention of sharing this information, now or ever.

It was enough that Gordon told her of his acquaintance with a girl in Williamsburg. She was glad to know it even though he did not state in any way that his relationship with Kitty was serious. If it was, why would he have courted *her*? That's most certainly what he was doing. She was sure of that. Wasn't she?

Angela took a seat at her desk and, without a response, waited to hear what Kitty was leading up to. She folded her hands in her lap, attempting to appear unconcerned by anything her visitor might say, even as her heart pounded impatiently for an explanation.

Kitty pulled up a chair to sit beside her. "I must tell you something in confidence. It is still a secret and no one must know. Even my mother doesn't yet know. Yet I feel I must tell you."

"And why would you tell me?" Angela didn't like confidences. Trouble followed them every time.

She prayed for Patsy and Jane to come bursting into the room. Surely this girl wouldn't want to continue with her little secrets in the presence of others.

But, she could tell by the animated talk going on up the stairs, that her sister and friend were happily occupied. Now, she wished she was with them.

The instant Kitty opened her mouth to speak there was a sharp rap on the door. Angela glanced out the window. There, to her surprise, was the very person Kitty spoke of. Gordon waited on the step, fidgeting with his hat in his hands.

Her stomach roiling from Kitty's near-confidence, her heart dancing at the sight of Gordon, she stood up. Putting a hand to her chest to still her thumping heart, Angela excused herself. "Forgive me but I must see to the door."

Kitty drew close to the window as Angela reached for the doorknob. Kitty gasped even before the hinge on the door had time to squeak.

"Angela." Gordon said her name as if he was reciting poetry.

"Good afternoon, Mr. Edwards," she answered pointedly. Gordon looked at her, confused. "I have a visitor with whom I believe you are acquainted."

"Hello, Mr. Edwards." Kitty stood at the entrance to the parlor, her hands clasped behind her back. She tilted her head and fluttered her eyelashes, in a bashful sort of way.

"Miss Baxter, I didn't know you were visiting Miss Harris." He looked, puzzled, from Kitty to Angela.

Kitty nodded. "I'm sure I told you I was visiting my cousin Jane. It turns out she lives right across the street from the Harris sisters. We've had a delightful time planning for the ball tomorrow night."

"And you are going to the ball, Miss Baxter?"

"Yes, of course, silly. That's why I came to Annapolis. Jane tells me it's the best night of the year. My mother and father are in town, as well." She put her hands out to clasp his. "I hope you will come and visit us while you are home. Mama would love to see you."

"Yes, I do hope that can be arranged." Gordon's pale skin took on a sickly pallor as he extricated himself from Kitty's clasp to return his gaze to Angela. "Miss Harris, I only came by to say hello to you and your sister."

"And here I am, keeping you standing in the hall. Please, come into the parlor and sit by the fire. It's quite cold today, isn't it? I'll go see where Mother and Patsy are. I know they'll want to see you. Kitty will entertain you. I shan't be long."

Angela rushed out of the room and then returned with a question. "Perhaps you'd like some tea?"

Already Kitty was taking a seat beside Gordon. Looking even more uncomfortable, he shook his head. "No, thank you. I can't stay long."

Angela sped up the stairs as well as her skirts would allow her. She didn't know what she was going to say and she didn't know how she was going to say anything with Jane in the room. Best to keep it simple, she decided.

"Mother, Patsy, Gordon—that is, Mr. Edwards—has just arrived. He was asking about you. I thought you might like to say hello." Angela struggled to keep emotion out of her voice and then she turned to Jane. "Mr. Edwards is an old family friend, you see."

She waited for her mother and then Jane to go down. Patsy grabbed her elbow. "What's wrong?"

"Oh, nothing," Angela hated lying to her sister. But she really didn't know what to think yet. "Kitty just told me that she is acquainted with Gordon. Nothing more, really."

"So she's his friend in Williamsburg?" Patsy stopped and looked at her with sadness. "Oh Angela."

As they all sat together in the parlor, Angela could see Gordon growing more uneasy by the moment during his brief visit. She knew she should feel sorry for him but, under the circumstances, she was content to see him squirm. She was suspicious that things weren't quite right. Someone was not telling the whole truth.

Was it Kitty, dreaming up a relationship with Gordon? She hadn't been able to share her secret—though Angela couldn't forget Jane's comment that she was engaged to a man whose name began with the letter G. Under these new and unusual circumstances, Angela really wanted to know what the girl planned to say.

Or—the thought stabbed at her—perhaps Gordon didn't tell her the whole truth. Was his friend in Williamsburg, in fact, his fiancee? If that were true, what was he doing here?

Gordon sat in the middle of the settee, with Kitty on one side and Patsy on the other. Her mother, always happy to join in a lively conversation, leaned forward from her favorite chair. Jane kept looking from Kitty to Gordon to Angela, as if she was trying to figure out a riddle.

No, Angela thought, something isn't quite right. Nevertheless, she had no intention of letting this girl get the best of her. If there was something serious between her and Gordon, she'd find out in due time. If it was all a childish dream, she'd be kind and feel pity for her.

For now, she listened politely as her sister and the other girls badgered Gordon with questions about school and the ball.

"Will I see you at the ball?" Kitty asked in a voice so sweet it gave Angela a toothache.

"Why, yes," Gordon replied. "My brother John has just arrived from Washington. He and I will be there with our mother and father. It's Mother's favorite event of the year."

"I simply can't wait," Jane chirped. "And wait until you see our dresses. Patsy and Angela just showed me theirs. Oh, but they are beautiful."

"You should come with us," Kitty turned to Jane, Angela and Patsy. "Wouldn't we make a merry party."

"I'm afraid we already have plans to go with Mr. Taylor next door." Angela was relieved she had an excuse to decline her invitation.

"And we are going with my brother," Jane added.

"Ah, just as well," Gordon responded. "I have the pleasure of escorting my mother tomorrow night."

Then he stood up. "I'd best be going now. I promised I wouldn't be gone long. Mother insisted I be home in time for supper."

Angela picked up the hat he had dropped on the hall table and handed it to him at the door. "I'm so glad I have had the pleasure to meet your friend from Williamsburg."

Gordon turned a bright pink. "Yes, well," he began. "Let me explain."

"Another time." As she spoke, she remembered the little charm. "I have something for you. Please wait a moment."

"Of course." He nodded.

Angela rushed up the stairs and drew the tiny gold charm from its place in her drawer. As she folded her hand around it, she had a sense of foreboding. She clutched it to her bosom and forced herself to descend the stairs in a more ladylike fashion.

"I believe this is yours." She held it out to him, willing her hand not to tremble.

"Why, yes it is. You wrote that you had found it. I'm so glad to see it again. Thank you, Angela." He caressed her hand as he took it, though his gaze never left her face.

"Please let me explain."

Angela shook her head. "It is getting late. We can't keep your mother waiting."

She pasted on her smile. Although she wanted desperately to hear what he had to say, she did not want Kitty eavesdropping in the next room.

"Very well. Thank you for this." He pursed his lips as he donned his hat and hurried down the steps.

In the parlor, Kitty and Jane were preparing to return home. Angela wasn't sure if she was glad or disappointed, especially since she was curious about Kitty's interrupted confidence.

The moment the door closed and the two girls were gone, Patsy turned to her sister. "Well?"

"Well?" her mother echoed. "Has something happened?"

"No, Mother." Angela frowned. "At least not yet."

"It seems little Kitty has her eye on Mr. Edwards," Patsy added with a wicked smile. "She is his friend in Williamsburg."

"Friend?" Mother turned to Angela. "Whatever does that mean?"

"Gordon told me he has met her on several occasions since he started attending William and Mary. Kitty seems to think—although she didn't tell me directly—that they have an understanding."

"They are planning to marry?" Mother looked alarmed.

"Neither of them has said anything of the sort." Angela felt her inner strength crumbling. She didn't know how to explain the unexplainable.

It must have shown on her face because Patsy's expression was filled with pity.

"Oh Angela," her mother said.

Chapter 12
Patsy's First Ball

The mail arrived as Angela and Patricia went upstairs to dress for the ball. Patricia started to turn to take the letters but stopped herself. She sighed and shook her head.

"I guess I've been silly. Even after all my letters were returned, I hoped he might see the error of his ways," Patricia said to her sister as they continued to their rooms.

"You've been steadfast in your loyalty to Mr. Stewart. After tonight, after you've danced and danced with all the young men, you'll forget Vincent's name," Angela replied.

Patricia knew her sister meant to be kind but how could she ever forget her first love? She trudged into the room they shared and slumped onto the bed. She glanced out the window though there was little to see on this wintry afternoon. The fields beyond their yard were barren, tipped with frost, colorless. The scene matched Patricia's mood. She knew she should be excited to attend the Winter Ball but it couldn't match her dreams. In all of them, she thought she would be dancing with Vincent.

Angela laid out their dresses on the bed beside her.

"They're so pretty," Patsy whispered.

Angela's was cut from a mossy green damask with wide lace adorning the scooped neckline. Patsy had chosen a pink silk gown with a rosy overskirt and dramatic puffed sleeves. Pale pink embroidered roses covered the skirt.

This, her first ball gown, was a gift from Uncle Max. She knew from the moment she saw the fabric it would make a beautiful dress.

"I think you should wear this tonight." Mother came into the room carrying her fine garnet and gold chain necklace.

"Oh, Mother," Patricia was breathless. Her mother treasured this necklace above all her jewelry. It had been a wedding gift to her from Father. "I don't dare wear that tonight."

"Why ever not?" Mother clasped it around Patricia's neck.

"What if I lose it?" Her fingers went to the stones, so cold and smooth. As thrilled as she was to wear it, she couldn't help but be terrified, too.

Mother nodded her approval. "It will look lovely with your dress. And I know you'll be careful."

Then she turned to Angela. "I have one for you, too." She held up a delicate silver filigree locket hanging from a black ribbon. "It was my mother's. She called it her treasure. When she was a little girl, she found it in the road behind her house. We've always wondered who it belonged to and how it got there. But she wore it all the time."

Mother looked at it and then looked at the collection of ribbons Jane had left behind.

"I was thinking you might want to exchange the black for something a little more cheerful," she said. "Ah this." She picked up a bit of ivory silk and held it against Angela's dress. "I think this would look very nice, don't you?"

"It's beautiful, Mother," Angela hugged her and kissed her cheek. "I wish you were going with us."

Her mother shook her head. "There's no place there for me tonight. I'd feel like I was in the way. Better for me to sit home and wait to hear all about it."

Patricia felt a lump in her throat as she hugged her mother. "It won't be the same without you."

Mother gave her daughters a warm glance and left them to get ready.

My first ball, Patricia thought. She held up her gown and touched the fine embroidery on the skirt as a hint of sadness crept into her heart. As excited as she was to wear this exquisite dress, as thrilled as she was to attend her first ball, she refused to let Vincent's shadow stealing some of the romance of this occasion.

It was really too bad Vincent wouldn't be there to see her wear this gown. But tonight, she refused to care. She was looking forward to the moment William led her onto the dance floor.

The hall was already crowded as they arrived, the air full of the sounds of the orchestra's violins. Patsy rushed into the ballroom, looked this way and that was she took in all the colorful dresses, glittering jewels, handsome men. She turned to say something to Angela, but found instead, a middle-aged matron beside her.

Where was she? And Jane, whom they'd met at the door? In the crush of the crowd she'd become separated from her friends. William had promised to meet her by the dance floor after he attended to their wraps.

She slipped past knots of acquaintances as they conversed, sidestepped couples on their way to the dance floor. She glanced at the buffet table, her stomach already rumbling. Candlelight danced across everyone's faces, making it difficult for Patricia to recognize her friends.

Again and again, she paused by the dance floor, looking for William. He'd been gone so long she was sure he must have been buttonholed by a business acquaintance or an old friend.

She strolled from room to room, looking for them all. As she went, she admired the high ceiling with its delicate moldings and the elaborate candelabra ablaze with light. She could smell the beeswax, the flowery pomades in the ladies' hair and the smell of sweat, horseflesh and leather.

With so many people jammed in, the hall was quite warm, inducing Patricia to retrieve her fan to cool her hot cheeks.

The sounds, the fragrances, the view thrilled her and eased her melancholy. Her sister and mother had gone over the protocol for accepting a dance or a cup of punch. She'd heard their warnings and their advice. The last thing her mother said as she kissed her goodbye was, "Enjoy yourself."

She was sure she would, if only she could find her friends and Angela.

She circled the ballroom again, this time staying close to the dance floor. Thinking she saw her sister, she hurried around to the other side. Then, she heard a laugh she was sure she knew well. She stopped and swiveled. It was a man's laugh and when she heard it again, she looked toward a cluster of people to see a man throw his head back in hearty merriment.

In the flickering light, and with others standing in the way, she couldn't be certain she knew the man's identity. But she'd heard only one person laugh with that deep joyous laugh. It had to be Vincent.

Her heart stood still and no breath would come. It couldn't be, she told herself as she struggled to retain her composure. It was impossible for Vincent to be here. He should be far away in Frederick. She craned her neck and strained her eyes to get a good look at his face. So far she had been unsuccessful.

If only people would stop getting in her way, she thought, as she took a step to her right. Her mother would disapprove of her staring but she needed to be certain. Impatiently, she waited until she could see the man clearly.

Look at me, sir, she willed him. But instead, Patricia watched in horror as he bent to kiss a delicate blonde on her upturned cheek.

She felt her knees buckle though she managed to stay erect. She fanned herself all the harder as she turned away from the scene she didn't want to see.

A pair of strong arms were waiting to catch her.

"Are you feeling ill, Miss Harris?"

Patsy clasped the man's arms, grateful for their support. "No, not really." Her heart skipped a beat when she looked up into the face of William Taylor.

His deep-set dark eyes were full of worry as he helped her to a chair. "You look like you saw a ghost."

"It's silly, really." Embarrassment burned on her face.

Mr. Taylor knelt on one knee before her, still holding her hand. "Not from the looks of it." He shook his head. "I was quite worried about you."

Angela rushed over and put her arms out to her sister. "Has something happened? Are you feeling ill, Patsy?"

Patsy shook her head. In a weak voice, she struggled to answer. "Vincent is here."

"Where?"

"Don't look!"

"But Patsy..."

"He's part of that group under the candelabra. Over there. He just kissed the lady beside him."

Patsy didn't dare look again but waited anxiously while Angela searched the room. As sure as she was, she hoped Angela would tell her she was mistaken.

Angela turned back and shook her head. "I don't see Vincent."

"I'm sure it was him," Patsy craned her neck so she could get a better look. Then, as luck would have it, the man with the wavy brown hair walked into a bright beam of candlelight.

Angela was right. It wasn't Vincent at all. He looked much older than Mr. Taylor. The blonde lady was more likely her mother's age.

Patsy giggled at her foolishness. She was embarrassed to have come so close to collapse, though she had to admit she was delighted to find herself in William's arms.

"It's hard to see who's who in the candlelight." Angela's voice was soothing.

Then William spoke up, his gaze following the sisters'. "Are you speaking about my friend Thomas and his wife Belinda? The man with the blue coat?"

Patsy answered him, feeling so foolish. "They are friends of yours? For a moment, I thought it was Vin— I thought it was a former suitor."

"Ah, I see." William turned from his friend to look at Patsy. "I'll have to introduce you."

He must have seen alarm registering on Patricia's face. "One of these days," he added with a kind smile.

Then he stood and held out an arm to each of the sisters. "Maybe the two of you would like some refreshment? There's usually a wicked wassail."

LOVE LETTERS & GINGERBREAD

"Mr. Taylor, how would you know that? I thought you didn't come to the Winter Ball."

He blushed as they walked through the throng. "It has been a long while," he admitted. "I used to come with my wife. Like you, Miss Patricia, she loved to dance."

Patricia's face turned a deep red. "I'm sorry. I shouldn't have teased you."

"No, I didn't mean to spoil your fun. It's just that it seems like she should be here." He was silent for a moment and then the light came back in his face. "My Juliet loved parties and she would be quite cross with me if she found me talking so sadly like this when I am in the company of two such beautiful ladies."

He led them to a large cut glass punch bowl at the center of the buffet table. Whole oranges studded with cloves bobbed in the amber liquid. Its aroma, of citrus and spice, scented the air.

Patsy took a sip of the punch, powerful with brandy and rum, and looked back to where she thought Vincent was standing. How could she be thinking of him when William stood beside her? She looked over the edge of her cup at him to see his eyes, now so merry, drinking her in. She smiled at him, her heart full of gratitude and affection.

She wondered how she had ever thought he was old. Tonight, all she saw was a charming, lively man. Perhaps he had lived long enough to serve in the war, to marry, and to have been widowed.

Tonight, he looked at her with such tenderness, she was delighted to be by his side.

The punch had warmed her, revitalized her after her silly shock. Now she wanted to dance.

As if he read her mind, William held out a hand. "May I have this dance?"

She smiled. "The pleasure would be all mine."

He bowed deeply and led her to the busy dance floor where the orchestra played a lively tune.

"I love the polka." Patsy placed her hand on William's shoulder. "Don't you?"

"I love any opportunity that allows me to hold a beautiful woman in my arms."

Off they flew around the floor until Patsy was dizzy and laughing.

As the song ended, William showed no signs of releasing her. Instead, he took the hand he held and kissed it, his soft brown eyes never leaving her face. Her heart leapt and she reveled in this new love. For that's what it was, she realized as she basked it his attentions. The moment thrilled her, if a warm sunbeam brightened the dark places of her heart.

She pushed aside all the hopes and dreams she once invested in Vincent. It felt as if she had just awoken from her worst nightmare to find herself in the presence of what could be.

Starting now she wasn't going to miss Vincent ever again. A world of music and dance awaited her.

The music slowed to a waltz, romantic and lovely.

"May I have this dance, too, Miss Harris?"

Patsy nodded and blushed. She looked up at him, gazed into those dark eyes and discovered she loved the crinkly lines that framed them. They signaled happiness.

For the first time in weeks, she really felt like dancing. She felt his hand firmly on her back as he swung her around. She had so looked forward to her first ball. Now, she knew, she would never forget it.

Chapter 13
Shall we dance?

Angela smiled at Patsy as she glided across the dance floor in William's arms. She was overjoyed to see her sister, despondent over Vincent's silence for so long, now looking so radiant. How could she feel anything but happiness?

Yet Angela wished she was dancing, too. She had hoped to spend the whole evening with Gordon. He'd promised to find her as soon as he could.

Rather than give in to her heavy heart, she tried to concentrate on the things that made her evening enjoyable. She'd been delighted when other gentlemen asked her to dance. She'd caught up with old friends she hadn't seen since their move. Still, she found herself continually scanning the crowd, looking for one man.

She chided herself for her impatience. Gordon had told her how much his mother looked forward to attending the ball with her sons. Of course, she would expect him and his brother to spend time with her.

Even so, she thought by now he'd have been able to get away. Where was he? Angela's mood grew darker with each passing dance. It was uncomfortable, finding herself without a partner in a room filled with revelers.

Patsy was in William's arms. Jane and Kitty had run off to speak to friends. Angela looked around for a way to not appear alone, abandoned. She opened her fan and lifted her head high as she took a turn around the ballroom.

She hadn't walked far when she spied Gordon. He stood not twenty paces from her in a shadowy corner. He didn't see her as he leaned over to speak to a matron swathed in black lace and silk. The scowl on her face was familiar. It could only be Henrietta Edwards. Beside her was another man who looked like a darker version of Gordon. She wondered if he was his brother John.

She suddenly realized someone else was there too. Was it Kitty? Could it be?

Angela walked on a little farther, trying not to stare, yet curious to see. It was Kitty. Angela had to admit she looked pretty in her pale blue dress and her hair piled smartly on her head with ringlets framing her smooth cheeks.

Kitty turned and caught Angela's eye with a smart little smirk and a shake of those curls. Then she entwined her skinny arm around Gordon's. Angela couldn't fight off the fingers of jealousy that clawed at her throat. She felt the blood run cold in her veins as loneliness set in.

Angela turned to walk the other way. Although Kitty had never had a chance to reveal her secret, the truth was clear. She did have an understanding with Gordon.

Feeling faint, Angela needed to get away from the stifling room. She rushed as fast as the crowd would allow, straight toward the exit for a breath of cold winter air.

New arrivals swung open the door and a wintry gust blew into the entrance hall. Angela inhaled all her lungs could take as the chill soothed her flushed cheeks. She put her hand to her forehead in hopes of easing the ache that lodged there.

The music sounded too joyful. The scent of perfume was too strong. She needed to get away from the laughter, the gaiety, the tender gestures.

"Angela." Jane appeared at her arm. "Why are you standing here all alone? You should be dancing."

Angela looked at her friend and laughed mirthlessly. "I wish I were but my would-be partner is deep in conversation and has another young lady hanging onto his arm."

"Kitty."

Angela looked at Jane, surprised. "Yes! How did you know?"

"As we were dressing tonight, Kitty confided in me." Jane hesitated for a moment. "She promised me not to tell anyone but I think you should know." She looked away and took a deep breath. "She plans to marry Gordon."

Angela gasped. "So it's true."

Jane looked at her in disbelief. "You already knew?"

"Kitty hinted at it. She said she was going to tell me a secret yesterday."

"But she didn't?"

Angela's head pounded all the more. "She didn't get the chance. I can't understand why Gordon hasn't said anything to me. He only told me she is a friend he met in Williamsburg."

Jane looked puzzled. "Kitty said she is planning on getting married in the spring and moving as far from Williamsburg as she can get. Oh Angela. Maybe it's not true. Maybe it's all in her imagination. Maybe he doesn't even know her plans."

Angela caught a glimpse of Gordon walking across the ballroom, his attention on the woman by his side. His mother this time, Angela noted, not Kitty.

Jane was a sensible girl. Perhaps there was nothing between Kitty and Gordon.

"Perhaps you're right."

Angela waited, hoping Gordon would see her. When he turned to greet another couple, she looked away. What she couldn't understand was why he hadn't come to her. Maybe she should have let him explain the previous day.

Her thoughts whirled like the crowd of dancers before her. Maybe when he called yesterday, he had planned to tell her he had become engaged. He wouldn't dare announce that in a letter. He'd have come in person.

It made perfect sense. When he finished his studies next spring, marriage would be a sensible next step. If that were so, that would explain why Kitty and her parents were visiting Annapolis, to meet her fiancé's family.

"Angela? Did you hear me?" Jane asked.

Her friend's voice broke through Angela's reverie. "I'm sorry. I got caught up in the music." She hoped Jane would forgive her fib.

Jane frowned. "I think there is something you're not saying."

"It's nothing, really." Angela sighed, unwilling to explain. Her feelings were in a jumble, her thoughts so confused. The only thing that would really help was Gordon at her side.

The next best thing was something to eat. "I'm getting hungry. Would you like to see what's on the buffet table?"

Jane recovered her happy demeanor. "Oh yes. I need the rest. My feet can't take another stomping."

Once their plates were full, they found seats in view of the dance floor. It was crowded with pairs following the lively steps of a reel.

Jane waved as Patsy and Mr. Taylor danced by. "I can't believe they are still dancing."

"I don't think Patsy expected such a lively dancing partner." Angela smiled at the sight of her sister's happy expression. Then she gasped and put down her fork, afraid she'd drop it when the room began to spin.

"Angela?"

She glanced at Jane and then returned her gaze to the dance floor, as Gordon danced by with Kitty in his arms. The two were deep in conversation so that he didn't even see Angela. He laughed at something Kitty said and then the little imp slid her attention from Gordon to Angela with that sly little smile she had perfected.

Angela refused to give Kitty the satisfaction of any reaction. Instead, she speared a piece of dark fruitcake studded with raisins and pecans with her fork. "This cake is delicious. Have you tried it?"

She put on her smile and vowed to remain calm. She refused to give Kitty the pleasure of seeing her upset. Their dance was of no concern to her. None at all. She had danced with several charming partners tonight and now she was enjoying a light repast.

It would have been a grand plan if Gordon hadn't spotted her. As he and Kitty danced past, he looked her way. With an expression of surprise, he stopped mid-dance. Kitty tugged on his arm and Angela turned her head to look the other way. She struggled to keep her expression neutral.

In mere moments, he was standing in front of her. He bowed. "Miss Harris."

Jane gathered her things and took Angela's plate. "I see someone I was hoping to talk to."

He quickly took the empty seat beside her. "Angela." He took her hand and kissed it.

All of a sudden, opposing emotions sprang up in her soul. How could she allow him such liberties after that display with Kitty? How could she let him leave?

"Mr. Edwards." Angela's heart was beating so hard she was afraid others in the room might hear it. She could hardly think of an appropriate response. Usually so practical in matters such as this, her heart had taken over the responsibilities of her brain. She had to think.

She was hurt. She wanted to forgive him. She was angry. She wanted to chide him.

Then her heart took control of her tongue.

"You snubbed me to dance with your sweetheart. I cannot complain. You are not bound to me in any way. You own me no explanations."

He recoiled, confusion clouding his eyes. "Sweetheart? But Angela, dear."

"Please, Mr. Edwards. I am not your 'dear.' " She wanted to get away but he held onto her hand.

"Angela—Miss Harris. I do apologize for my late arrival. My mother had several people she wanted me to meet. And then, just as I was beginning to look for you, that Kitty insisted we dance."

"Yes. I saw you. As I said, you owe me no explanations. Now if you will excuse me. Go, enjoy yourself."

Then she rose without a word and walked away. Her hands shook so badly she clasped them in front of her. She didn't know where she was going but blindly passed through the throng of people.

In a quiet corner, she gulped air and wrung her hands as she chided herself. "I shouldn't have spoken that way. I really shouldn't have."

Now regret fought with despair for a place in her wounded heart. Angela closed her eyes and struggled to contain her feelings. It would do no good for others to see her in such a state.

Once her heart quieted, she composed her face so no one could tell she was mortified. Angry. Hurt.

She couldn't return to her seat and risk meeting him again. She found Jane sipping punch beside the buffet table.

"Oh there you are." Her friend handed Angela her plate. "What happened? Gordon was in quite a state."

"Was he?"

"Did you quarrel?"

Angela shook her head.

"No. But I do believe I can't stay. I do hope you'll forgive me."

"Yes, of course. What shall I say if I see Gordon—or Kitty?"

"Only that I was feeling ill. Or, better still, could you find Patsy?" Angela stopped herself the minute she said those words. "No, don't. I don't want to ruin Patsy's first ball. Now will you please excuse me?"

Happy in William's arms, Patsy caught sight of her sister speaking with Gordon. Relieved to see them together, she twirled with the other dancers. Then, exchanging partners with another couple, she lost sight of her sister. It was only a moment or two before she could see Angela again.

Was she crying? And where did Gordon go? When Angela rushed out of the room, she pulled William off the dance floor. Her heart went out to her sister, sympathetic to her hurt feelings. "William, I think Angela needs to go home. I hate to leave but could you take us?"

She led him toward the entrance hall, anxious until she found Angela. She was standing alone, waving her fan wildly before her flushed face.

Patsy rushed to her. "I saw you talking to Gordon. Are you all right?"

"Yes, I'm fine." Angela's voice didn't sound right.

"Perhaps we should go home. William has agreed to take us."

Angela shook her head. "Nonsense. I don't want to spoil your evening."

"Angela. I think it's time to go."

"But Jane—"

"Jane will find Kitty and her brother and some young man who has been waiting to dance with her."

"You and William—"

"Are exhausted. We have danced our feet off."

William arrived with their wraps. "Are you ready?"

Angela nodded. Patsy took her arm and led her to the carriage.

The ride home was silent as a tomb. Patsy kept hoping Angela would talk to her but she kept her face turned away. Patsy longed to offer some words of comfort but she kept quiet. Better to wait until they were alone, she decided.

After their ball gowns had been laid aside and the pins were out of their hair, Patsy climbed under the covers with her sister. "I'm sorry about Gordon."

Angela turned over with an inscrutable look. "There's nothing to be sorry about."

Patsy searched her face for the hurt she knew was there. "He treated you quite badly at the ball. It should have been your night and instead, he spent almost the whole time paying attention to his mother and some girl he hardly knows."

Angela's look only grew stonier. "He owed me nothing. We are only friends. If I thought we might enjoy the night together, I was mistaken. Gordon's mother needed him and Kitty is an old friend. He tells me they've been acquainted for some time."

Patsy was alarmed by her sister's expression and her words. She didn't understand. Angela's face showed no sadness and her words were empty of feeling.

"I really don't want to talk about it, Patsy. If I had hopes of getting to know Gordon better, I don't think that will happen now. It's best not to think of it—of him—again."

She turned her head into her pillow but not before a single tear slipped from the corner of her eye.

Patsy's heart went out to her sister and she wanted to cry big fat tears for Angela, so ill-used. She couldn't understand why Angela wouldn't tell her what happened between the two of them. Angela had to know she, of all people, would understand the pain of a disloyal lover.

Patsy sometimes still thought of Vincent, but she didn't miss him anymore. Tonight she had well and truly given her heart to William. She rolled over and thought of him. She admired his kind eyes, his considerate ways, his love of poetry. Yes, he was different from Vincent but there was no denying he was a good man, kind and sensitive, always thinking of her. He had an inner fire that she knew would keep her warm all of her life.

William was still in her thoughts as she drifted off to sleep.

Chapter 14
Too quiet

Angela didn't know what to say, how to explain. So, morning after the ball proceeded, she said nothing. She tucked her mother's necklace back in its proper place, remembering with disappointment how she let her emotions get the best of her. She should never have allowed Kitty to make her jealous. And angry.

She carefully folded her gloves and shawl to store away in her highboy as she remembered how she'd spoken so harshly to Gordon and left him standing there alone.

The scene replayed again and again in her mind as she tended to her ball gown. Even as she knew better than to let her feelings control her, she couldn't shake the despair and loneliness that weighed her down.

Then she slumped onto her bed, trying to make sense of her conversation with Gordon. When he came to see her, she refused to accept his apologies. Instead, she answered with cold words and a stony look.

"You owe me no explanations," she had said. "Go, enjoy yourself."

Angry and in pain, she had left him without even giving him a chance to explain. She'd glanced back only one more time. Only once but it was long enough to see coolness in his eyes replace any affection he had earlier felt for her. Something registered in his face she had never seen before. Maybe it was relief. After all, perhaps on that very night he planned to announce that he was going to marry Kitty. That would be a perfectly reasonable explanation for why he stayed away. It would have been an awkward moment. One she was glad to avoid. She realized she had no cause for making demands on his attentions. Theirs was only the briefest of friendships. Hardly worth a notice.

At breakfast, Angela didn't know what to say to Patsy. Or her mother. So she said nothing.

As she sat with her sister and mother, she didn't feel it was right to reveal anything about the secret engagement Kitty alluded to and Jane announced.

Unable to explain as she sipped her tea, she refused to allow her emotions get the best of her. Even if she couldn't deny her jealousy the previous night—It had made her speak in a hateful way—this morning, she had to rein in her feelings. Until then, silence was the better course.

She considered for a moment sending an apology for her incivility to Gordon. She sat at her desk with a sheet of paper in front of her. She was at a loss for words. Maybe, she thought, she should be waiting for Gordon's letter of apology to her. Overcome again by her emotions, she put the paper away.

She leaned her cheek on her hand and tried not to think about the ball. About Gordon. About Kitty. About what she said. About how she felt.

She stood up, restless. Angela didn't ever remember feeling so unsure of what to do next.

"Angela?" Patsy peeked into the parlor, a look of sympathy in her eyes. "Mother and I were wondering if you would like some company. It isn't good for you to suffer alone like this. You haven't spoken all morning."

"I haven't? Oh, I'm sorry."

Mother bustled in and wrapped her arms around her elder daughter. "It's been too quiet in here. I expected a house full of chatter today. But, under the circumstances…" She held Angela at arm's length and studied her face.

"I haven't been crying, if that's what you think."

"Crying? Oh my dear girl, I wouldn't expect that of you." She drew her daughter to the settee. "But do tell me all about the ball."

Patsy followed and sat across from her sister and took her hand in comfort.

Angela still didn't know what to say. Though she preferred to say nothing at all, she felt she did owe her mother an explanation.

Angela forced a smile, weak though it was. "The ball was delightful. Even if it wasn't what I expected at all, Mother. But I'm glad Patsy had an enjoyable time with Mr. Taylor."

"So I gathered. Patsy has talked of nothing else. Mr. Taylor is quite a nice man."

"Nice? Is that the best you can say?" Patsy asked.

Their mother looked confused. "Should I say more? I thought you were still yearning for Vincent."

"No. Not at all." Patsy jumped up to twirl about the room. "That story is over. I do believe I have fallen in love with Mr.—with William."

Angela studied her sister's face as she returned to her seat and saw she was speaking the truth. Patsy was never good at invention. No, she wore her heart boldly on her sleeve.

Their mother smiled. "Oh, well, that is good news. I'm so pleased. Mr. Taylor is quite a lovely man. I do believe his interest in you is sincere."

Patsy nodded. "We had such a delightful time last night. He surprised me with his dancing abilities—and his fortitude. I should have expected to grow tired from all that dancing but not with William. He spoke so sweetly, I could never get tired."

Then she grew serious. "I did have a moment when I thought I saw Vincent. But I was mistaken. That was the only time all night that I thought about him. William was so charming."

Angela was glad the conversation centered on Patsy and her newfound romance, rather than her conversation with Mr. Edwards.

However, once her mother seemed satisfied with Patsy's reporting on the ball, she turned her attention to her elder daughter. "You haven't said a word about Gordon since you came home. Did you have a quarrel? Is that what happened?"

Angela had dreaded this moment. Patsy, bless her heart, spoke up. "You should have seen her, Mother."

Patsy looked at Angela with a sympathetic expression. "She was so patient and kind as she waited for Mr. Edwards. His mother kept him by her side for almost the whole night. Then when we finally saw him, it was after he danced with another girl. With that Kitty."

Angela started at the girl's name. Still she said nothing. She didn't feel quite right revealing the couple's relationship since it still hadn't been publicly announced. Although that dance surely was public enough, Angela still felt the need to keep mum.

"He then asked Angela to dance?" Mother asked.

"Yes, he did but by then I was quite unwell. The room was hot and my shoes pinched." Angela stopped and looked down at her hands.

"My heart would have been too broken to dance," her sister interjected.

"Oh no, it wasn't like that." Angela shook her head. "There's no reason I should be his first or only dance partner."

Patsy stood up, a look of disbelief on her face. "But he asked you to promise him a dance, remember. And, Angela, the way he looks at you when you are together, he must love you."

Angela wished she would stop but still Patsy went on. "How can you be so unfeeling about the slight you experienced? Your heart should be broken. Your face should be covered in tears. I can't believe—"

"Patsy, I don't believe Gordon loves me as anything more than a dear friend." Angela knew how she felt. But she also knew what Kitty had told her. And what she had seen the previous night. Her love for Gordon would always be unrequited.

"But surely you are in love with him, aren't you?" Her mother put her hand on Angela's. It was cold and Angela shuddered.

"I don't know." Angela's voice was small and she hoped her face didn't reveal her torment. All she knew was that she had fallen in love with a man who had promised to marry another woman. It was best she not admit what she felt.

"Oh Angela." Patsy sat beside her sister, her voice softer. "Even I know. Your feelings are written all over your face from the moment he walks in the room. There's no denying your feelings. Or Gordon's."

Angela's hand shot up to her hot cheek. She sighed a little sigh and shook her head. "Under the circumstances, I don't think it prudent to hope for anything more from Mr. Edwards. He has his schoolwork to think of and he is much too busy even to spend a few minutes writing letters." She worried her words were too sharp but it was the best she could manage.

She could see the impatience in Patsy's expression. "Prudent? This is no time to be sensible, Angela!"

Angela laughed at her sister. "I think this is exactly the time for prudence."

A knock at the door relieved Angela of continuing her conversation. Patsy jumped up and peeked out the window. "William is here. Shall I ask him in or would you prefer not to have visitors?"

"Yes, of course." Angela could see the glow of delight on her sister's face as she danced off to answer the door.

Angela's mother looked pleased as she prepared to greet their guest. "I think someone new has finally won your sister's heart."

William entered the room and bowed. "Mrs. Harris, Miss Harris."

"William has invited us to take a ride in his carriage," Patsy said. "And he brought in the mail."

Angela thanked him and took the letters. Out of habit, she rifled through them before putting them on the secretary. She gasped at the last one: It was addressed to Patsy. She pondered whether to give it to her sister right away or save it for after their carriage ride.

William was urging the family to join him. "It is surprisingly balmy for December and since we don't get too many days like this in winter, I thought perhaps we should take advantage of it."

Angela knew she would not be good company and declined the invitation. She slipped Vincent's note in her pocket.

Her mother stood to see the couple to the door. "What a considerate gesture, Mr. Taylor. You two go. I'll stay back here and keep Angela company. Go enjoy yourselves."

Once the party had bundled up and rushed out the door, Angela returned to her desk. Her mother came up beside her and put a gentle hand on her shoulder.

"Will you be all right, Angela? If you'd like some company, I'm happy to sit with you."

"Thank you, Mother. I'm fine. Really."

"Nothing more you want to say? About last night?"

Angela shook her head. Perhaps Patsy would have wailed about the transgressions she experienced last night. But Angela didn't want to do that. She preferred to hold her roiling emotions in check, hard as it was. It was better to do something than sink under the weight of her feelings.

"I have this mail to read. I think that's a better way to spend my time don't you think?" She hoped her face looked brave and strong as she spoke.

Her mother bent down to kiss the top of her daughter's auburn head. "You know, my dear. Love isn't only a feeling. It's an action, too. I see you express your love for us and for Gordon in your every action."

"You do, Mother?"

"I think he'll come around. He'll see that your love is powerful."

Angela felt the world get a little brighter. Love is a feeling and an action. "Thank you, Mother."

"Now you see to your correspondence and I'll see what Ella's up to." Her mother glanced back with a hint of a smile before disappearing down the hall.

Angela didn't pick up a pen or open any of the letters. Instead, she drew the note out of her pocket, leaned it against the cabinet's drawer and wondered what news it contained. Secrets were terrible— she could hardly stand the pain of knowing Gordon and Kitty's. But sometimes it could be worse when a secret was revealed.

She worried about what was in Vincent's letter, about the truths it might contain. She leaned her cheek on her hand to think. It was too quiet.

Chapter 15

Her fate is sealed

As Patricia and William settled themselves in his carriage, her little dog Timmy jumped up on to the seat and wedged himself between the two. Then he put a paw on William's leg and looked up at him.

Patsy laughed. "He's waiting for you to pat him. It's funny. Timmy doesn't usually like men. He was downright grumpy with Vin—with a friend of mine."

William gave the little dog a good scratch about his ears and then turned his attention to driving. "When I was very young, I remember that my grandmother used to have a dog who was also named Timmy. I loved that dog. I remember him as really big but now I realize it was I who was very small."

"You never had a dog of your own?"

William shook his head. "No. I was young when my mother died. Then I went to live in the orphanage. That's no place for a pet."

Patsy laid her hand on William's arm. "Of course. I'm sorry I mentioned it."

"Oh, no. My memories of the place are good ones. Although I would have liked to have a known my mother better."

"My mother never wanted a dog. She always said she was too busy without the bother of a dog. Then when I found this little fellow last spring, I begged her to let me keep him. And she agreed."

William glanced over at her pup and, as he give its ear another scratch looked up at Patsy. "He's a good little pup. I imagine he's a good companion."

Patsy nodded with a smile, her heart welling up at the affection William showed her pet. Timmy had been a true comfort when she was so keenly feeling the loss of her father and again in these recent months since Vincent's departure. How lonely she would have felt without Timmy's affectionate face to cheer her up.

When she looked at William, she felt certain she'd never feel that pain again

William drove out into the countryside, past rolling fields shorn of their crops or dotted with cows and chickens. The bright winter sun peeked out from pillowy clouds and turned the landscape a deep gold.

William said little as he drove and his silence puzzled Patricia. He was a quiet man who seemed unperturbed by the lack of conversation. He seemed content simply to have her by his side.

Patsy, on the other hand, was bursting with questions. She knew so little about him. Only that he was an orphan. He had served in the army and worked with her uncle. Could he still play a drum? What were his late wife and child like?

She knew, too, he was a good man, a trusted business partner and friend to her uncle.

And, she smiled as she wiggled her toes, he was a tireless dancer.

As the carriage bumped along, she commented on the weather, the scenery, even the horse, looking for something that would prompt William to speak.

He responded with great courtesy, offering a comment or two of his own as they traveled out and finally turned back toward town.

Then, she remembered the book of poems he gave her. "I was reading some of the poetry book you gave me."

"Yes? Did you like it?"

"Oh, yes, I did. Very much. I love how much the poet can express in so few words."

He seemed to consider her statement for a moment. "It's almost as if poets know how to paint a picture."

"The emotion of poetry, its passion, its depth of feeling…doesn't poetry make you feel alive?"

"Oh yes." He nodded and glanced at her. There was something he wasn't saying. Patsy hoped by continuing the conversation she would encourage him to reveal more about himself.

"I think poetry is life. I not only read it, I write it. For me, it describes the very essence of our souls."

He nodded again as he looked down the road. To Patsy, it seemed as if he looked deep into the past. "You sound like my late wife."

Patsy started. She hadn't meant to elicit sorrow in William. "I'm sorry," she started to say.

"No. I only meant she and I used to read poetry in the evenings. For me, it was only a pleasant way to while away a few free moments. But Juliet brought the verses to life. I didn't value them as more than pretty sentences, some of them indecipherable with all their allusions and turns of phrase. When she read them to me, I could see their power."

Patsy stared at her companion, awed by his words, touched by his feelings for his wife. "I would like to have known her."

He turned to her then, his face full of tenderness. "She would have enjoyed knowing you, too."

Perhaps it was forward of her, but she couldn't help it. She tucked her hand in his arm. "I'm glad to know we have a love of poetry in common."

"I must admit I haven't read it since…well…I came across that book and thought you would like it. As for me, those little rhymes no longer have a purpose ."

"Purpose? Poetry doesn't need a purpose. It merely needs to be read and loved."

William nodded. "Then perhaps we should read together."

Patricia thought of all the hours she spent scribbling lines in her little notebook, reading the works of Cowper, Turnbull and Shakespeare. Her father loved to hear the sonnets. She would have to make time to share what she loved with William.

"Certainly, you must know this one." Patricia sat up straighter and spoke out: "'Is love a fancy, or a feeling? No. It is immortal as immaculate Truth.'"

As he pulled the carriage in front of her house, William turned to her and smiled. "It's a beautiful sentiment. But it's new to me."

Patricia stood up, surprised that a man of some learning and experience didn't know it. "It's Coleridge! I read it in the book you gave me."

He jumped from the carriage and held out his hand to help her down. "It is? I've forgotten."

"Then I shall have to read it to you and remind you of its beauty." She detected in William deeply-felt emotion, lost love, sorrow and then, when he looked at her, she knew he had hope, too. Hope in a future with her. "Yes, we must read it together. Poetry is life, William, all the experience of life distilled into verse."

She gathered up her dog and took William's hand, warm and strong. She wished she could look inside this reserved man and discover all the secret thoughts and emotions he kept locked inside.

He held her hand to his chest. "Thank you for a delightful afternoon. I will study my poetry this evening so we can talk about it tomorrow."

Satisfied by their conversation, and the hint at the memories he held close, she smiled. "Oh yes. Tomorrow at dinner."

"I look forward to it." He kissed her hand tenderly before letting her go.

Patsy slipped inside the house and ran to the window to watch with new eyes as William drove off. Then, inspired by their conversation, she rushed across the empty parlor to the secretary shelf where she kept her poetry books. As she reached to open the cabinet door, her eyes fell upon a letter addressed to her.

The room faded away as she focused on the note she had longed for. She could hardly breathe even as a voice inside warned her that this was no request for forgiveness. It would, no doubt, tell her only what she already knew.

Timmy danced at her feet, begging for her attention. She stooped to pick him up before taking a seat near the window. Her dog's cold little nose nuzzled her chin as she willed her pounding heart to settle.

The note was brief. Not the usual pages and pages of news about the family, a visit with friends, and finally flowery declarations of love and affection.

"Dear Miss Harris…" Those were words to strike fear into a true romantic's heart. And then came the words that sealed her fate.

"Circumstances require that I inform you of my impending marriage. As it turns out, I will not be returning to Annapolis. Please forgive me but I shall not write again. Yours, Vincent."

Patsy couldn't help allowing his name to slip quietly from her lips. "Vincent." The words blurred on the page as she tried to reread them.

Her mother and Angela flew into the room.

"Vincent's letter!" Angela pushed the dog off the sofa and sat beside her sister.

Her mother hovered, wringing her hands. "What does he say, dear?"

Patsy couldn't even repeat the words. She could barely see her mother and sister through the tears flowing down her face. She handed the note to Angela and collapsed into sobs. Mother knelt beside her and wrapped her arms around the poor girl.

Patsy didn't want to hear Vincent's words again but she couldn't stop Angela from telling Mother the news.

"He's getting married."

What horrible words! Patsy cried all the harder.

Mother and daughter clung to each other and sobbed. "Married! Oh my poor Patricia. How could he cast you off like that?" her mother cried.

Ella rushed into the parlor, a wooden spoon still in her hand, and looked from sister to sister. "What happened?"

Patsy looked up, tears burning on her cheeks. "Vincent..."

Angela handed Patsy a handkerchief. As her sister blew her nose, Angela explained what Vincent had written.

"Is that all? I thought someone died," Ella huffed.

"Patsy expected Vincent to ask him to marry her," Angela explained.

Patsy sighed and choked back the tears that threatened to come again.

Her mother wiped her own eyes. "If you had seen him. We were sure of it."

Ella poked her spoon in the air. "You're getting yourself all upset over a man who hasn't written to you since you moved here. It may not be my place to say so but I think you should be getting worked up over that nice Mr. William. He's a good man. He's an honest man. He'll be a good husband. Now I best be getting back to supper."

The sisters and their mother looked at each other.

"I can't believe she said that to me," Patsy said.

Angela patted her sister's hand. "She's right, you know. Miss Ella is a sensible woman."

"I know. I really do." Patsy smiled weakly at her practical sister before taking the crushed letter from her mother's hand. "But I can't help how I feel. Seeing these words makes it so final. He was my first love. At least I thought he was." She reread Vincent's words with a heavy sigh. "Everything he said was a lie, wasn't it? Did he mean nothing he said, nothing he wrote in all those letters?"

"I'm sure he meant every word," her mother cooed. "He wouldn't have led you on that way if he didn't think you two had a future."

"Future? I suspect he went to Frederick and never thought of me again. I wonder if he went knowing he would become engaged to that lady?"

Patsy felt a swirl of emotions, ranging from pain and sorrow to confusion. And then betrayal. She excused herself and trudged up the stairs to her room. The sound of Timmy scurrying behind her offered some comfort.

She threw herself across her bed to cry again. Timmy lay beside her, his face fixed on hers. When she could cry no more, she sat up and pulled her dog into her lap.

"I knew it all along, didn't I?" He cocked her head and nodded at her. "You knew, too, didn't you? You didn't even like him. And he never warmed up to you. The silly man. How could anybody not love and adore you?"

She crumpled into tears again as she hugged little Timmy. "How could he not love and adore me?"

When the tears were gone, she stared up at the old fashioned canopy, her eyes following the swirls of gathered fabric as she absent-mindedly patted her dog. The news had exhausted her, left her feeling empty.

When she met Vincent so soon after Father died, she found such comfort in his company. Now, all she felt was empty and used. And thrown away. She'd stayed true to Vincent for so long.

"Is love a fancy or a feeling?" She whispered the line she'd earlier quoted to William.

William.

She remembered how he looked at her with such affection as he held her at the ball, as he took her hand to help her in the carriage, as they sat side by side at dinner and today during their carriage ride.

She would waste no more fancy, no more feeling on Vincent. She had a lot to learn about love. And William.

She crumpled the note and tossed it on the floor.

CHAPTER 16
CHRISTMAS EVE

"I really don't want to talk about it." Mother's tone was sharp. She and Ella were in the parlor setting up the table for the Tannenbaum.

Ella was quick with a response. "I don't like to repeat gossip. But I thought you might want to be prepared. I was thinking of the girls."

Angela could hear the argument all the way in the kitchen where she and Patricia were stringing popcorn to wind around the tree. Her curiosity got the best of her and she left her sister to stroll as nonchalantly as she could into the parlor. After all, they could be talking about her or Gordon.

She strolled in, trying to effect a cool demeanor. "What gossip?"

Angela didn't like the troubled look on her mother's face.

"I better get the nuts and apples." Ella rushed away, her lips pursed.

Angela picked up a cookie to hang on a limb. "Has something happened, Mother?"

Her mother waved away the question with her hand. "It's probably nothing."

"Let me decide if it's nothing. It has you bothered."

Mother turned to look at Angela, though she did not reply.

"Has something happened?" Angela disliked repeating the question but all she could think of was what the town wags might be saying after that scene at the ball. She knew the news of Vincent's impending marriage must also be racing through drawing rooms all over Annapolis.

She hated the idea of either her sister or herself being the topic of local gossip.

Her mother took a chair by the fireplace. "Sit down, dear."

Angela's breath caught in her throat as she obeyed her mother and then put her hand on her flushed cheek. "Something is wrong, isn't it?"

She could tell from her mother's frown this wasn't about Vincent. This was about Gordon. And the ball. And Kitty.

She hadn't seen either Jane or Kitty since the ball. Both were invited to help trim the tree this afternoon—but so far, neither had come. Truth be told, Angela was certain she never wanted to see Kitty ever again.

"It's only a little thing," her mother finally said. "Kitty was sent home after the ball. Her parents packed her up and took her back to Williamsburg the next day. Ella just told me she heard people talking about it when she went to the market this morning. No one has said why but everyone is imagining the worst."

Angela was liking this conversation less and less. "And what would that be?"

"I wish I knew. I hope it isn't something to do with the ball."

Angela felt her heart flutter. "Do you mean Kitty and Gordon? Or Kitty and Gordon and me?"

"As I have said, I don't like gossip."

And now her head hurt. "But, Mother, what is being said about me?"

"Oh, Angela."

But she had to know. "Mother."

"There has been talk that Gordon went after Kitty, that they plan to be wed in Williamsburg."

Angela laughed it off though she wanted to cry. "Oh, now really, Mother."

"So you are not concerned?"

Even as her heart sank, Angela had no desire to lie to her mother. "I have no understanding with Gordon Edwards. I like him. I enjoy his company. But there has been no discussion of anything beyond friendship. I knew he was previously acquainted with Kitty. Although

Gordon never intimated that there was anything serious between them, Kitty hinted at that before the ball. Then, their actions at the ball demonstrated to me that I need not bother myself with the likes of Mr. Edwards again."

"And?"

"There's really not much to add." Angela felt the loss of her friend deeply but the day before Christmas was supposed to be one of anticipation and joy. For the past week, she had gone over again and again what happened and finally realized she had jumped to the conclusion Gordon might be in love with her.

Every day she felt like Patsy waiting for the mail to arrive. Just as her sister had looked forward to a letter from Vincent, Angela found herself expecting to hear from Gordon.

Nothing came. Not a letter. Not a visit. Only silence. She did not want to burden her mother with her woes.

Her mother fiddled with the ribbon she used to tie the cookies to the Tannenbaum. "I can't help but worry. It's a mother's prerogative to protect her daughters."

Angela kissed her mother. "You are a dear."

Going about the business of preparing for Christmas was going to be difficult on this cold, snowy day. But even as her heart ached for Gordon, Angela was determined that this Christmas be happier than the one the family let pass unnoticed last year. She knew how important this holiday was for her mother and sister, finally recovering from their grief.

So she focused on the tree. This was the first they decorated in many years. She smiled and hummed a Christmas tune, an old but cheerful song her father used to like. Then she picked up the molded gingerbread ornaments and tied them one by one on the fragrant boughs.

Mother joined her, both in trimming the tree and in humming the tune.

Angela took a step back to admire their work. The Tannenbaum held a place of honor on a mahogany table near the fireplace. Tiny white candles were attached to the limbs ready to be lit tonight. "It really is a beautiful little tree."

LOVE LETTERS & GINGERBREAD

Her mother looked up from the bowl of nuts Ella had brought. "Uncle Max found a fine tree, so full and fragrant."

Angela suddenly missed her uncle. "Why isn't Uncle Max here?"

"He said he had to attend to something at his shop after he finished putting on the lights." Olivia adjusted the slim white ribbon on one of the gingerbread cookies. Then she turned to Angela.

Patricia came in bearing a long string of popped corn. "I finally finished. Shall I put this on now?"

"We usually put it on first but now will have to do." Angela examined it with a frown. "It's not very long."

"Yes, I know. It should have been much longer but I burned one batch of corn." Color rose to Patsy's face. "And then I ate some."

"It looks like you ate a lot. I should have known better than leaving you alone in there." Angela shook her head. She didn't mean it, though. Her sister's mood had brightened considerably now that she knew the truth about Vincent.

In fact, Patsy had surprised her. The morning after receiving Vincent's letter, she rose early and dashed off a letter of congratulations to her former suitor. She arrived at the breakfast table, waved her letter and declared herself free of any feelings for him with a shake of her head. Not that she was fully recovered. She did, after all, announce she would never again tolerate hearing Mr. Vincent Stewart's name.

Patsy welcomed William into the house with devotion. He continued to come every day at dinner and with each visit, her affection for him was ever more evident. She danced to the door when she heard him knock and sat a little too closely if Mother wasn't in the parlor. The previous day, she wrote a poem for him late into the evening and tucked it into a box of the traditional German cookies. She planned to share it with him after supper on Christmas Eve.

She approached Christmas preparations with new enthusiasm. She'd joined in the baking of the stollen and the pfeffernüse and wrapped presents to send to Uncle Karl.

Angela was happy to see the color back in her sister's cheeks as they wound the popcorn string around the tree. When they were finished, the sisters stopped to admire their handiwork. "It needs a little more popcorn," Patsy said.

"Oh no," Angela objected with a laugh. "We have plenty to decorate the tree."

While they were still laughing, Ella came in with a visitor.

"Jane!" Patsy ran over to embrace her friend but Jane hardly hardly looked at her, entranced as she was the partially decorated tree.

"Patsy! Angela! It's beautiful."

"Wait until you see it with the candles lit," Patsy said.

Mother handed Jane the bowl of apples. "Patsy will show you how to hang these."

As she tied a bow, Jane looked from Patsy to Angela to their mother. "I suppose you've heard."

Ella clucked her disapproval of gossip as she brought in cups of cider.

"Oh, Miss Ella, this isn't just gossip. This really is true." Jane's eyes grew wide and she leaned in. "Gordon has left town. My brother is a friend of his brother John. He told me there was a terrible row the day after the ball. He caught the next stage to Williamsburg."

Angela suppressed a gasp as she wondered if he was chasing after Kitty. "What could possibly have made him leave now?"

"I don't know. But I suppose you've heard Kitty went home with Uncle James and Aunt Penny."

"What's this?" Patsy wasn't privy to the earlier conversation. "Has Gordon gone after Kitty?"

Angela didn't have the heart to answer. Feeling a little sick she found her way to a chair.

With a look of horror, Patsy looked at her sister. "Oh no, Angela."

"It's gossip, girls," their mother reminded them. "We don't know what caused Kitty to go home. We don't know why Gordon left. Everything else is only a fairy tale."

Angela didn't feel any better. She really didn't know how to feel. She quickly dismissed a twinge of guilt. She couldn't have had a part in what had happened after the ball. She'd behaved as honorably as she could—especially after Gordon's snubbing. That's what it was, after all. He'd chosen his mother and a girl he called a mere acquaintance over her.

If she didn't feel guilty, she was certainly angry. As angry as she felt as she stood by the dance floor seeing the man—to whom she'd given her heart—dance with another woman.

She longed to retire to her room. She needed to sort it all out and decide if there was something she should do.

Uncle Max burst into the room, bringing in a gust of cold winter air, and a dusting of snow on his coat.

"Merry Christmas, girls," he said, his voice booming with his customary joy. He kissed his sister. "Merry Christmas, Olivia. I am the luckiest man alive to have a house full of such lovely women this Christmas. Most Christmases, I'm nothing but a lonely old bachelor."

"You are nothing of the sort, Max," his sister retorted. "Except for last year, when we were not in the mood for making merry, you always spend Christmas with us. And last year, Karl reported the two of you celebrated the season with great conviction."

Max laughed heartily. "I can always count on Karl to tell stories! I'm sorry, my dear sister. Would it be better to say I've never seen my parlor look lovelier. Beautiful ladies, beautiful tree!"

"Much better," she said and crossed the room to kiss his rosy cold cheek.

Then Max said, "I've asked William to dine with us tonight. He accepted with alacrity."

Angela glanced at Patsy whose happiness radiated in her eyes. She was glad for her sister, glad she was finding happiness this Christmas.

❄ ❄ ❄

The ladies chatted, telling Jane stories about the family's past Christmases, as Max lit the candles one by one.

"The tree is beautiful," Jane said. "I can't believe everyone doesn't have one of these in their parlor. I told my mother I wanted a Christmas bush but she just laughed at me."

Max chortled. "When you are all grown up, you can trim a tree for your own family. Children seem to like the things."

"So do you, Max," Olivia said.

"So do I, Uncle Max," Angela said as he lit the last of the candles. "It brings a little gladness to the soul, doesn't it?" She couldn't help but smile as the tree shimmered with candlelight.

Jane rose and paused for a moment, her cheeks golden from the tree's light. "I think your idea is a grand plan, sir. And now I must hurry home. Mother will be expecting me."

Once she had hurried off, the room was quiet as the family admired the tree. Patsy sighed as she listened to Ella's singing in the kitchen and the crackle of the fire.

A knock at the door brought William into the festivities. Patricia stretched out her hands to draw him into the family circle. Now her happiness was complete as she saw the look of affection in his dark brown eyes. "Merry Christmas, William. We just lit the tree."

He tucked her hand in the crook of his arm as they stood before the tree. He nodded but looked at her instead of their *Tannenbaum*. "So you have. It's beautiful."

When William turned to look at the tree, Patsy looked at William. She had truly learned to love this man. He might not have the romantic style of Vincent, but he was generous, attentive, gentle.

She had discovered his love of poetry and of music and dancing. Surely they were signs of a romantic heart. In the past week, they had spent time reading poetry together. William had even memorized the Coleridge poem and recited it to her on one afternoon when he was able to linger after dinner. Her heart soared at his efforts.

He was steady and true—two things Vincent most assuredly had proven he was not.

The light of the candles lit a spark in his dark eyes. They really are handsome eyes, Patricia thought as she bid him to sit beside her on the settee.

No sooner had he settled in when Ella called the family in for supper.

William kept a firm grasp of her hand and whispered to her to stay back while the rest went into the dining room. Her mother glanced her way, and with a hint of a smile, nodded.

Once the room was theirs alone, he drew a small flat package out of his pocket. "I wanted to give you this. Merry Christmas, Patricia."

She looked up from the brown-paper-wrapped parcel to William. She was touched.

"Please, open it." He urged her.

She untied the silk ribbon and unwrapped the gift. "Another book?"

She ran her hand over the small leather-bound volume of Shakespeare's sonnets and realized this wasn't just another book of poetry.

William gently took it from her hands. "I bought it because I thought you would like it." He opened it to the title page. "There's an inscription."

He had written in a strong hand: "We all want to fall in love. May you fall in love with me as I have with you. Your William."

Patricia stared at the page, gently touching it with her hand. She was never so moved.

Then she looked at the man who wrote those lovely words. "William," she whispered. "Is this true?"

"With all my heart." His eyes were warm. His voice was soft. He took her hand again and kissed it even as his gaze never left her face.

With her free hand, she clutched the book to her heart. "It's the most wonderful gift I have ever received. Thank you."

"I know how you love poetry." His gaze was as soft as his voice.

"It's not only the book. The inscription. What you wrote. Your love!" She struggled to express how she felt.

"I know you have been pining for a certain young man. I know you may not be ready to love me. But I am hoping that day will come when you are able to love me. I am willing to wait." He looked down at their entwined hands. "Even if I have to wait forever."

"But how did you—?" She began and then blushed. "Uncle Max..."

He shook his head and smiled a little. "I'll never betray a trust. But I must ask. Will you think about it? Even a small hope would be the greatest gift you could give me."

She searched his eyes and realized all he said was true. "Yes. My heart did belong to another. I have only found out... I now know my feelings were misplaced."

William's eyes searched her face. "Does that mean…?"

She nodded. "You have my heart, dearest William."

As she said the words, she was certain that she meant them. He had shown her a depth of feeling that was honest and good. Vincent had regaled her with a romance that wasn't true. Or that couldn't last. She knew she could trust William to take care of her heart.

"You have made my Christmas very happy, my dear." William leaned toward her. "May I?"

Patsy suddenly realized he hoped to kiss her. She met his gaze, soft with affection for her. She was touched and felt her heart flutter.

No, he wasn't the impulsive gentleman Vincent was. But in that moment she was certain he was a man who wanted to make her happy. Would there be passion? She didn't yet know. But he surprised her tonight. Perhaps he would surprise her again.

She leaned in to touch his soft, warm lips with her own.

There in the flickering light of the *Tannenbaum*, Patricia felt his strong arms embrace her. This felt so different from Vincent's kisses. But it felt right to be in the embrace of such a caring man. She felt the rise and fall of his chest as he sighed with satisfaction. How good it felt to make William happy. How good it felt to be loved.

It wasn't the Christmas she thought it would be. And yet, she felt hope and joy tonight, on this happy Christmas Eve.

CHAPTER 17
CHRISTMAS DAY

Angela removed her bonnet and smoothed her hair. The aroma of bacon wafting into the entrance hall should have made her hungry. Yet, she couldn't imagine eating.

She had woken early—on Christmas Day of all days!—feeling almost as sad as she did on the day of her father's funeral. She had felt such a sense of loss on that awful day.

She didn't ever think she could bear another day so painful and yet here she was, feeling some of that same loss and emptiness.

Her sister and mother kept quiet on the way to and from church. And she felt guilty about that. She knew her pain was etched on her face. She could feel the dull thud of a headache that seemed to stretch all the way down to the frown she couldn't prevent.

While the others hurried in for a hearty breakfast, she stayed behind to settle her feelings. As she hung up her hat, Ella approached her with her most beautiful smile. "Frohe Weihnachten! Merry Christmas, Miss Angela," she said. "Breakfast is ready. Everybody's waiting for you."

"Thank you, Ella. I'll be right in."

She adjusted the sleeves of her dress and straightened her grandmother's filigree heart at her throat. Forcing a happier expression, she entered the dining room and took her place at the table.

Uncle Max's warm greeting was the only sentence spoken as the family tucked into a festive breakfast. Angela knew she must say something. It was Christmas morning after all.

"The sermon today was especially moving, don't you think?"

Patsy handed a bit of bacon to the dog at her feet. "Was it?"

"Weren't you listening?"

Patsy's fork hovered over her plate as she answered. "No, I had too many things on my mind. After the Christmas story, I must have stopped paying attention."

Uncle Max chuckled. "You wouldn't be thinking about a certain gentleman."

Patsy blushed. "Oh, Uncle Max."

Angela couldn't help but smile a little. Patsy had forgotten all about Vincent. Now her heart belonged to William. Her longing and pain had turned to hopefulness when William announced his love for her. There would be wedding bells soon. She was overjoyed at the news.

Angela moved the food around on her plate and sipped at her tea. Happiness was important. Even though she had thought she found a bit of her own, she had become resigned to the fact that it was now out of reach.

She listened as the others chatted about who was visiting today as well as plans for getting supper on the table after Ella left to visit with her family. She had to admit, it was good to hear the excitement in everyone's voices.

Last year, the day had passed without any mention of visitors, gifts, supper. They'd gone to church and come home to a cold breakfast. Mother spent the day in her room, a handkerchief at the ready. Patsy and Angela occupied their time by reading and sewing.

The only reminder of the holiday was a package from their uncles, sent from Karl's home in Sharpsburg. Though it arrived a few days early, the girls decided to save it for Christmas Day. Then, after unwrapping boxes containing candies, madeira and books, they composed thank-you notes to be dispatched the next morning. It was such a melancholy day compared to today's merriment. And yet Angela didn't have the heart to join in fully.

Ella appeared at her elbow. "Angela? You have a visitor. He's waiting in the parlor."

Angela looked up at Ella and then at her family, all with their eyes on her.

"Who is it?" She didn't wait for an answer. She knew who it

was and stood, steadying herself as she put her napkin on the table. "Excuse me."

She walked slowly, deliberately down the hall as she tried to sort out her feelings. She was wary, unsure of his objective, even as new hope took root in her heart. After all, she didn't know what had ensued after the ball. She only knew snippets of gossip.

Her breath hitched as she entered the parlor. There sitting by the Tannenbaum, and looking most uncomfortable, was Gordon. As she crossed the room, he rose and bowed to her.

"Merry Christmas, Angela!" His tone was as formal as his bow.

She curtseyed when she longed to clasp his hands.

"Merry Christmas, Gordon. Whatever are you doing here? I heard you went to Williamsburg. I thought—"

"Please," he said and bid her to sit beside him. "I am filled with sorrow and regret for any pain I might have caused you. That night got away from me and I was most insensitive to your feelings. I certainly did not mean to keep you waiting." He bowed his head. "I am ashamed to admit, however, that is exactly what I did. I'd promised to dance with you. Instead, I kept you waiting."

He drew a little package from his coat pocket and presented it to her. "I've brought your a small gift. It is only a token. I spied it in the market and thought of you."

Angela looked at the gift and then at Gordon's face, full of penitence and regret, before she tore off the paper.

She chuckled at the sight of the tin gingerbread mold. It was so similar to the ones used for the decorations now hanging on their Christmas tree.

He looked uneasy as Angela admired at his gift. "It's an angel," he explained "When I saw it, I thought of you. I know it's not much."

She looked up at him with a smile and tears in her eyes. "You thought of me? But, Kitty…"

"Please, don't mention that name. I don't know how to make amends for my behavior." A crease appeared between Gordon's pale eyes. "I do hope you'll forgive me."

"But—" Angela was confused.

"Please, dear Angela. Say you'll give me another chance. My

actions at the ball were unkind to you. You have every right to be angry with me. I didn't intend on snubbing you."

She shook her head. "I shouldn't have been so cross."

"Yes, you should have. It was unpardonable. My mother insisted I stay near, as she is wont to do. Perhaps you aren't aware how she expects her family to surround her at all times. That night she kept my brother John and me on display for all of her friends. I should have told her you were waiting. Truth be told, I never had someone waiting for me before." A hint of an uneasy smile crossed Gordon's face as a blush bloomed in his fair cheeks. "

He went on to explain that as soon as his mother dismissed him, Kitty arrived and pulled him into a gavotte. "I regretted my weakness the moment I saw you."

Silently, he slipped his hand into hers and looked at her with some hesitation. She allowed it, her heart softening at the sight of the sorrow in his eyes. Then she waited for him to continue with his explanation.

"It must have felt awful, standing there alone when I promised to dance with you. For my actions I am truly sorry."

She nodded. It had been a terrible moment. But she wondered if perhaps she was too hasty in her actions. "I can see my words were too harsh."

"No, please, my darling, I have come to seek your forgiveness. You owe me none at all. Please forgive me for that distressful night. I hope I can make it up to you."

"But Kitty—"

Gordon recoiled. "Kitty means nothing to me."

"I was led to believe you rushed off to Williamsburg after her parents took her home. I took that as a sign of your true affection for her. She confided in me that the two of you planned to marry once your schooling was finished."

Gordon laughed. "She told my mother that, too. And my mother, let me assure you, was none too pleased."

He told her how Kitty shared her secret with his mother during tea the next day.

"In fact, I was preparing to come see you, to apologize then, when my mother summoned me. I wasn't even aware of Kitty's presence in the house. By then, Kitty had already been asked to leave, assured that no marriage would take place."

He sighed deeply and shook his head. "I promise you, Angela, I never considered marrying her. We were only acquaintances in Williamsburg. Any plans for marriage were nothing but a dream of her own design."

Still, Angela wasn't completely convinced. "But then why did you go to Williamsburg?"

Gordon explained that his row with his mother ended in an ultimatum: that he never socialize with Kitty again.

Her demand prompted Gordon to make his own wishes known. It was time to stand up to his mother's directives. He needed to set his own path. "I agreed that I would never see Kitty again but then I told her of my own decision. That I was withdrawing from William and Mary."

He said he didn't wait for her reply. Bolstered by newfound courage, he dashed out of the house and caught the stagecoach to Williamsburg. Not to see Kitty, as the town wags whispered, but to gather his things and quit school there. "To be honest, I wasn't even aware Kitty went home. Nor did I care."

The roads were so full of snow and ice the trip was slow and arduous. Finally, he realized he might miss Christmas at home—with her—if he continued on his journey. He got off and took the next stage back to Annapolis.

He gazed into her eyes, searching for the forgiveness he hoped she would give him. "I only returned late last night. I could hardly sleep, waiting for the morning to come so I could come and see you. I had to, if only to give you the angel and to apologize. The past week has been so topsy-turvy and I regret not visiting sooner. I'm sorry for the pain I've caused you."

Even with such a penitent expression and those apologetic words, Angela couldn't decide how she felt. Even though she was no longer angry or envious, the pain deep inside her lingered. He'd put his mother's—and Kitty's—desires above hers. She couldn't answer him, afraid of what harsh thing she might say.

So she said nothing.

He reached for her hand. It had become a familiar, welcome gesture. Now, though, she didn't give it to him. So he tucked it in his pocket. "Please, you must forgive me. I've thought of nothing except you. You gave me the courage to do what I had to do."

She started. "What do you mean? I gave you courage?" It was about time, she wanted to say but chose not to.

He nodded with his eyes cast down. "I've been a fool. I was letting others run my life. I know I ought to honor my parents. But it's time make my own way in the world. You made me see that."

He reached for her hand again. "Please, can you ever forgive me? I promise I'll never do anything so egregious again."

This time his words eased the pain in her heart. She nodded and allowed him to wrap her small hand in his large one. "Of course I'll forgive you.

He sighed and kissed her knuckles. "That is very good news. Now allow me to share my news."

She dipped her head, curious for him to proceed

"I wrote to the college upon my arrival home and told them I will be be returning in the new year. Then I wrote to my landlord to notify him of my change of plans. I did assure him of course I'd be back after the New Year for my books and things."

Angela didn't understand why he was leaving William and Mary. He was nearly finished with his studies. It couldn't be only to avoid Kitty. "Why aren't you going back?"

"I've withdrawn to start medical school in Baltimore."

Angela saw the pride in his face and clapped her hands. "Oh, Gordon. You got your wish!"

Gordon beamed a glorious smile and then his expression grew serious again as he recaptured her hand.

"Angela, I had two wishes this Christmas. One was for my career. The second was for my heart. Both will ensure a happy future. You, dearest, gave me the courage to take the first steps toward becoming a doctor, a desire of mine for so many years. And now, my second wish, the one for my heart, rests entirely with you."

Her heart danced at his words, at the emotion he expressed in his face. "Do you mean…?"

He nodded. "The thought of losing you made me reconsider everything. I can't go back to William and Mary when my heart is set on becoming a physician and caring for the sick."

"Yes, and now so you shall."

He folded her hand between both of his and shifted in his seat so he faced her directly. The breath caught in Angela's throat as he searched her face. "But that isn't enough for me. Not now that I know you. I must spend my life in the company of a wonderful woman. I want to spend it with you, if you'll have me."

Angela stared at him in amazement—as a collective gasp echoed from down the hall.

"I don't need an answer right away," he said when Angela didn't respond. "I only know I love you."

"Dear, dear Gordon," Angela whispered. She gazed into his loving eyes and nodded. "I can't imagine life without you."

Gordon swept her into his arms and kissed her by the light of the Christmas tree. "Merry Christmas, my dearest," he whispered into her ear.

Angela hugged him to her heart. "I can't imagine one happier."

The End

Afterword

What was Annapolis like in 1831? Still a small village, its activity was centered on its harbor. Even though it was the capital of the state of Maryland—its State House is the oldest capitol in continuous use in the nation—it was no longer the center of the country. Congress which gathered here in 1783 was now meeting in its own Capitol in young Washington D.C. Furthermore, the U.S. Naval Academy that now dominates much of Annapolis life wouldn't open for fifteen more years.

West Annapolis was not as far west as the current West Annapolis. And where it ended farms began. Surely Angela and Patsy would have felt like they were living at the edge of civilization.

I look plenty of liberties. The house where I imagined Dr. Harris had his thriving practice on Prince George Street is actually the former home of Thomas Jefferson's physician, which is now an elegant bed and breakfast. (I visited several times as a writer for Frommer's travel guides.) Imagining the west Annapolis house of Uncle Max was a bit more difficult since the area has grown and developed a lot since 1831. I dreamed up the Winter Ball, too. Jane Austen's characters are always going to balls so I had to organize one for Angela and Patsy.

I studied furniture and clothing of the era so the young woman would have places to work and dream and correspond with their young men, and pretty clothes to wear on occasions such as that imaginary ball.

Finally, the poetry quoted here is contemporary to the era or was published early enough to be available to my characters. I've used the same poem by Hartley Coleridge, son of Samuel Taylor Coleridge, that Marianne quotes in the movie starring Emma Thompson and Kate Winslet, as well

LOVE LETTERS & GINGERBREAD

"Love," penned by the elder Mr. Coleridge. A swoon-worthy poem quoted in Chapter 3 was written by Samuel Woolworth, an American poet who lived briefly in Baltimore. That seemed a natural for my Maryland-based novella.

❦❦❦

This holiday love story of Patricia and William and Angela and Gordon wouldn't be the same without the help of great people.

First I must acknowledge my gratitude to my fabulous critique group who read it first: Alexa Jacobs, AR Case, Kimberly Butler, Ivy Quinn, Kristie Wolf, Nellie Jane, and Rose Harris. They encouraged the story from the first paragraph.

Thanks to Megan Tilghman for creating the book's beautiful cover.

And, finally, I am so very grateful to E. Elizabeth Watson who offered to read my book and then, not only provided some great advice, but honored me by writing the lovely recommendation that appears on the cover.

Many thanks to you all.

You've read the prequel. Now don't miss

DIVIDED LOYALTIES

Eighteen-year-old Maureen saw soldiers once before. As a little girl in County Galway, she watched British soldiers patrol near her father's pub. Maybe she didn't understand "the troubles" then.

But now, as Union and Confederate troops converge near Antietam Creek, she yearns to serve her adopted country. Let her friends laugh. Let her father demand she remain at home. Maureen is determined to find a way. A new battlefield hospital might provide her with a way to be of service. How hard can it be to work as a nurse? She's about to find out.

Maureen is too young. Too inexperienced. Yet she's tenacious and devoted. To succeed she must overcome self-doubts, stand up to her father and the young soldier who loves her and face dangers she couldn't imagine, even staring down the wrong end of the gun.

**Second Edition Paperback
available from
Amazon.com
and
BN.com**

**E-book for Kindle and Kindle Unlimited
still available from Amazon.com**

Chapter 1
MARCH OF SOLDIERS

The pounding steps of soldiers echoed through the valley. These troops were the first Maureen and Joe had seen marching by their farm. Maureen usually loved the sound of visitors outside her door. These men, marching from parts unknown, were strangers, and they brought fear—fear and the specter of war at their doorstep.

She couldn't help watching them as she and her brother Joe fixed the fence near the road. Most marched in neatly-formed columns, a model of military discipline, looking neither right nor left as they passed.

Maureen looked at her brother as his brown hawk-like eyes followed the troops until they marched out of sight. She knew his heart and spirit were with them. He wanted to join the fight.

"Something's brewing." Joe turned away from the road. "When I was in Sharpsburg this morning, there was talk of a Confederate occupation. It's not gonna happen, but you know how people are. It's all they talked about. Some were packing up and going farther north."

While he was talking, more troops passed by, this a rag tag band of men who stopped for a sip of water from the nearby creek, laughing and shouting to one another.

Maureen bristled at their coarse language.

"Don't pay them any attention, Moe," Joe whispered, and returned his attention to his work. "They're just showing off."

"They're the scruffiest lot of soldiers I ever saw," Maureen muttered. "Confederates! What are Confederates doing here?"

She frowned and crossed her arms. When one of them grinned at her and winked, she scowled at him and looked away. He was not the sort she'd want to run into on her way to town. He was cocky, and with a gun he would be downright dangerous.

The thought made her shiver.

"They want to provoke us, Moe. Ignore them." His dark eyes slid away from his work to the soldiers as they continued on their way. He set his jaw as he shoved the last rail firmly into place and then he climbed to sit on the mended fence.

"It all seems so familiar, doesn't it, Joe?" Maureen rested her arms on the fence and looked up at her brother. Joe nodded, his focus fixed on the now quiet road. Maureen wasn't sure he was listening.

"Like the British soldiers we saw in Galway," he finally answered. "I was thinking of that, too. I'll never forget Old Man Murphy. He'd shout every time a soldier walked past his house."

"The men at the pub used to get so angry at them." Maureen remembered how, night after night, the townsmen gathered for a pint in the small pub her parents kept on the road to Galway. As the peat fire grew smokier, the conversation usually grew louder. Always, they ended the night complaining about the British soldiers.

"It seemed like more and more marched through town as time went by," she said.

Joe shoved his hands in his pockets and shook his head. "They said the British Army was an occupying force. But this is different. This country is at war with itself."

Maureen knew Joe was anxious to enlist. He'd begged his father for permission for months though Father wouldn't hear of it. After their father had been injured in a fall earlier that summer, Joe had taken on running the farm.

All the while, Maureen knew Joe had never given up his intentions to enlist.

The two of them, born only a year apart, had been inseparable for as long as they could remember. Maureen couldn't imagine life without her strong-willed brother.

It was clear he was determined to go, and soon, now that Father was nearly well. She only wished she knew how she could serve her adopted country, too.

"No use thinking about it now," Joe said. "You better go see that the chickens aren't out. One of those soldiers might decide to liberate them." He jumped from the fence and stomped off toward the orchard, anger evident in his wiry frame. Maureen rushed to the hen house in the back yard. With relief, she saw her favorite, a black hen with a white diamond on her chest, leading the rest toward Maureen, cackling non-stop.

"Here you go." Maureen spread feed on the dusty ground. She hadn't thought about hungry soldiers stealing her chickens. She'd have to keep an eye on them.

She relished the peaceful moment as the chickens pecked away at their food. Both she and Joe had worked hard to keep the farm running these past few months. Besides her farm chores, she had helped her mother care for her father—not an easy task when her father grumbled every waking moment. She understood his pain and frustration. Summer hardly had a chance to begin when he fell through the shed roof. Now the season was in full bloom and the corn stalks in the fields stood taller than Joe. She knew how disappointed Father was that he'd missed it all.

"Nice to have nothing to do."

Maureen turned to see her brother's friend Patrick sauntering up to the henhouse from the road. She held her tongue, much as she wanted to tell him all she'd done that very morning. She'd tended to her chickens, drawn water, lit the fire, made the coffee and the oatmeal, re-bandaged her father's wound, brought him his breakfast and listened to him go on about her incompetence yet again. She'd helped Joe in the cornfield and had spent the last hour with him repairing the fence.

Instead, she greeted Patrick with an unimpressed sigh. "Hello, Patrick." She crossed her arms. "Joe's not here. I saw him head toward the orchard a while ago."

Patrick's pale baby face turned deep red. "What makes you think I was looking for Joe?"

"Why else would you be here?" She wasn't in the mood for his tiresome flirting. He flirted with every girl. Though Maureen longed for a beau of her own, she knew his flirtations were meaningless.

"You're right, of course. I was looking for Joe. We were going to see about joining the army today."

Maureen stood up straight, the chickens forgotten.

"Today! Before Father's recovered?"

"We're not leaving today. We just wanted to find out what we have to do to enlist. I wouldn't leave without saying goodbye to you." Patrick's eyes twinkled and she knew he was teasing her again.

"Go on with your blathering, you eejit." She put her hand on her hip and frowned. She found her brother's friend a little annoying. "You're all ready to leave?"

"Yes, I am. I figure I'm enlisting no matter what Joe decides. I don't want to miss the war. The people in town are saying it might not last until the end of the year," he told her.

Maureen was figuring out how to respond when she saw her friend Eliza duck under an apple tree branch and skip down the well-worn path between their two farms. Usually neat as a pin, she had bits of grass in her hair and mud on her white muslin skirt. Maureen smiled with relief when she saw her, a welcome distraction to Joe's tiresome friend.

"Where have you been?" Maureen reached over and pulled a strand of grass out of her best friend's long blonde braid.

Eliza laughed and looked own at her clothes. "I was…helping mother in the garden. I guess I look a mess."

"Indeed, you do," Maureen said.

Even dirty, Eliza couldn't help but be pretty. With her golden skin, long yellow tresses and perfectly oval face, she was the opposite of Maureen. Her mother always said Maureen and her brother were Black Irish like their father. Her eyes, dark as night, glowed in her square face. Although her unruly curly hair was nearly black, her skin was so pale it sunburned the moment she walked outside. She barely reached five feet while her willowy friend was a head taller.

Though Eliza and Maureen called each other cousins, their connection was only by marriage. Uncle Raymond, a distant relation to Maureen's father, had come to the States long ago, met and married Priscilla Riley and adopted her two children Robert and Eliza.

"How'd you escape your father's sick room?" Eliza asked.

"Doctor Lee was here this morning. He told Father to get out of bed, and you know Father. He started one of his tirades. When he decided to go on about my inadequacies, Mother—bless her heart—sent me out to help Joe."

She stopped a minute when she heard her father's growling filtering through the back door. She listened until she heard her mother answer his call.

"So, Patrick says he's signing up today," Maureen continued. "I wish there was something I could do to serve. I'd go in a heartbeat."

Eliza laughed. "A girl in the army—" She stopped when she saw Maureen's face darken. "You're serious, aren't you?"

"Right ye be," Maureen replied. "I'm not saying I want to take up arms, but there must be some way I can serve. This country welcomed us when we were forced to leave Ireland. It was scary at first. So many strangers who didn't talk like us. Then one night I lay in my bed and listened to the crickets. It was then I realized I was home. Here there was peace, freedom and a whole new family to love. No more soldiers on patrol. No more angry men dreaming of independence. This country is my home now."

Her friends stood silently for a moment. Then Patrick had to interrupt. "But it's a man's job to protect it. That's why we're taking up arms." Although his frown looked serious, Maureen couldn't miss the twinkle in his eye as he added his last jab. "You womenfolk stay behind to keep the home fires burning."

"Really now, Patrick Toohey? Is that our job?" Maureen glowered at Patrick. "The cheek of ya."

Joe sauntered toward them from the front of the house, a half-eaten apple in his hand.

"Moe's spouting off again, isn't she? I heard ya. She can be right gabby when she wants to be."

Maureen threw her hands up in exasperation. "Don't you be siding with Patrick!"

Joe laughed. He elbowed his friend in the ribs. "Been catching a little heat from my sister?" When he caught sight of Eliza, he dropped his apple as he blushed. "Hello, Miss Brennan! How are ya?" He bowed with an awkward flourish.

Maureen shook her head at them all. "I've had just about enough from all of ya." She wiped the dust off her hands and started back toward the house.

"Come on, Maureen," Patrick said, a sly smile crossing his face. "Can't you take a little teasing? We don't mean no harm."

"Don't mind her. The soldiers have set her off," Joe said and clapped his friend on the shoulder. "You all ready to go, Pat?"

Patrick nodded solemnly.

"My brother has already left," Eliza said. "Amy begged him not to go—they've barely been married a year. You know how conscientious Robert is. He told her he was duty-bound to enlist. Then he brought her to stay with us while he's gone. She's done nothing but mope about the house, poor thing."

"You heard about Zack and Tom?" Patrick asked.

Joe shook his head. "What eejits. Gone and joined the Confederate Army."

"Their pa's a Southern sympathizer. The Hendersons have lots of family in Virginia," Patrick explained.

"Doesn't make it right," Joe muttered.

"They're following their hearts just like you." Maureen knew soft-hearted Tom well enough. She was sweet on him for the longest time though he never noticed.

"Are they now?" Joe's eyes were full of scorn.

"What about you, Joe?" Patrick asked. "Ready to go?"

Maureen saw a look of alarm pass over Eliza's face. Maureen knew without Eliza telling her that she had developed quite an attachment to Joe.

"I hafta talk to Father one more time. If he says no… I'm not sure what I'll do."

Maureen understood the despair in her brother's voice. He loved his new country the way a convert loves his new church. He was fervent in his love for America. When Uncle Raymond used to tell stories of General Washington's celebration of St. Patrick's Day during the Revolutionary War, Joe ate it up. His ardor was catching; Maureen was inspired by Joe's retold stories. Like Joe, she longed to do anything she could to bring peace back to her beloved valley.

Plenty of their friends had already left. She longed to do something besides watch them all leave.

Mother appeared at the kitchen door. She nodded at Maureen.

What does Father need now? she wondered.

"I've frittered away enough of my afternoon," she told her friends. Then she looked pointedly at Patrick. "I have home fires to tend to."

"I'm sick of corn," Joe told Maureen as they walked between rows of towering green cornstalks. The silk on fat ears of corn had darkened, a signal that harvest was near.

"Patrick's been gone a month now. So has Robert. All the lads are gone, and I'm still stuck in this field." He shook the hoe he carried and thrust it out in front of them. "I could take this hoe and throw it in the creek. I don't care what happens here anymore. Not when there's a war going on. Not when I can hear cannon fire so close to home."

"I understand," Maureen said and pulled the hoe out of his hands. Then she put a hand on her brother's shoulder and smirked. "You're sounding like the men that used to shout in the pub."

Joe laughed and nodded. "I guess I do. I didn't know what the fuss was about in those days but I heard the passion in their voices."

"It wasn't passion. It was the effects of the beer you were hearing. All hot air and nothing more. Nothing has changed in Ireland since those days," Maureen said.

"True enough. And yet I do believe the day will come when Ireland will be free."

They had arrived at the end of the cornfield as it opened onto the hen house and the apple orchard. In the quiet of the afternoon, they could hear cannons firing in the distance.

"They've been going at it all day, Moe," he told his little sister. "I've heard the fighting since first thing this morning. And if you look, you can see smoke rising off South Mountain."

Maureen shaded her eyes from the strong September sun and looked across the valley, a half-day's walk from their farm. "How long can it last?" she asked.

Joe looked toward the mountain and said nothing.

"Joe?"

He nodded without looking at her.

"You're thinking the fighting will come here?"

"No doubt about it," Joe told her. "The soldiers we've seen in the past few weeks? I don't know where they're planning to fight but it sure looks like it might be near here. Here or Shepherdstown. Maybe Harper's Ferry. We've seen too many soldiers for the fight to be too far off."

Maureen looked at the mountain in the distance. "Patrick isn't there, is he?"

"No, it's too soon. None of the boys we know are there. They've got training to do before the Army will put them into battle. Either Army— you know the Henderson boys headed South."

Maureen nodded.

As Joe fell silent, she wondered what he was planning. Father's objections had been vehement. No matter what Joe said, Father shot him down. He'd spat out only disgust at Joe's patriotism, reminding him that loyalty to a nation had led their family to heartbreak and their exile from Ireland. He'd reminded him of his duty to his family and the farm. He'd asserted his authority as head of the household. All of it only strengthened Joe's resolve.

Maureen could see Joe's desire to enlist in his face. He stood there in silence, his eyes trained on the rising tower of gun smoke. His hands were shoved deep inside his pockets—the jingle of coins a sure sign he was planning to go soon. He wouldn't listen to his father's yelling ever again.

Maureen didn't know what to say. She rested her chin on the hoe handle and memorized this moment with her brother. Maybe he'd already made his decision. Maybe this would be the last day they spent together. Even though she hated the thought of seeing him leave, she couldn't ask him to stay either. She had so many things she wanted to say. She longed to tell him that she'd miss him, she loved him, and she'd pray for him every night.

Suddenly, he seemed to awaken from his trance and turned to her. "I suppose Mother is looking for you for help with supper. I'll take the hoe back and—and then I'll be in."

Joe stared at Maureen for a moment as if he was going to say something more. Instead, he took the hoe from his sister and waited to watch her head into the house.

Later, when Maureen put a bowl of potatoes on the table for the evening meal, Joe was nowhere to be found. She called up to the loft for him to join them at the table. She had started for the back door when that she realized Joe wasn't coming in for supper. He was probably on his way to Hagerstown. She looked at her mother and father who waited in silence as if they already knew Joe was gone.

Her mother shook her head. "It's no use, Maureen. I've already looked everywhere for him. He ran into the loft a while back, but I paid him no mind. I'd like to think he's headed to town or over to Patrick's house. Then I remembered Patrick's gone, too. And Robert."

"And Zack and Tom," Maureen murmured. Everyone had left except Joe, and now it looked like he was gone, too.

"The Henderson boys?" her mother asked. "But Mrs. Henderson told me…"

"They crossed the river and joined the Confederate Army."

"Enough, ladies." Her father stretched out his hand to his daughter's seat. "Maureen, sit down and let's have our supper. If Joe's gone, so be it. If he hasn't, then he's late for a very good meal."

Wordlessly, Maureen sat in her place across the table from Joe's empty seat. Before she could answer, her mother shot her a warning look. Instead, she picked up a fork. Supper passed without a word. Maureen saw the grief in her mother's eyes. Her father sat stone-faced, staring into his empty teacup long after she and her mother had cleared the table.

Joe didn't say goodbye.

Maureen's heart ached for her stubborn, brave brother. She knew it might be a long time before they saw him again.

Even though it hurt, she was proud of him. And envious. *Joe left to serve his country,* she thought. *Why does it matter that I'm a girl? I can't stay here and do nothing when there's a war going on.*

About the Author

Mary K. Tilghman, a Maryland native, has spent 40 years writing for local newspapers and magazines. In addition, she wrote six editions of Frommer's travel guide for Maryland and Delaware and one edition of the *Insider's Guide to Baltimore*.

Mary's first novel *Divided Loyalties* was published by Black Rose Writing in 2017. Set in Sharpsburg, Maryland, during the Civil War, it follows an Irish immigrant as she sacrifices family, friends and comfort to serve as a battlefield nurse working in a tent hospital.

The e-book for Kindle is available at Amazon.com. The second paperback edition is now available at Amazon.com and BN.com.

Divided Loyalties was cited in CBSBaltimore's "Five Baltimore Authors To Put On Your Summer Reading List." It also received Four Roses in a Romance Novel Addicts Anonymous review.

Mary is a member of the Romance Writers of America, Maryland Romance Writers and the Historical Novel Society.

She and her husband Ray have three grown children and a 22-foot sailboat. And more deer in her yard than she could ever want.

Keep in touch—
Find news about Mary's latest projects at
www.MaryKTilghmanWrites.com

Twitter: @maryktilghman

Facebook: @MaryKTilghmanWrites